(DYING IS FUN)

Opening the Door to the Future

In recognition of a gift to the
Falmouth Public Library Foundation
for the
Falmouth Public Library

From

Eugene & Arlene Rubin

Thank You!

Also by

Vladimir Nabokov

novels

short fiction

Drama

The Waltz Invention

Lolita: A Screenplay

The Man from the USSR and Other Plays

Autobiography and Interviews

Speak, Memory: An Autobiography Revisited

Strong Opinions

Biography and Criticism

Nikolai Gogol

Lectures on Literature

Lectures on Russian Literature

Lectures on Don Quixote

Translations

Three Russian Poets:
Translations of Pushkin, Lermontov, and Tyutchev

A Hero of Our Time (Mikhail Lermontov)

The Song of Igor's Campaign (Anon.)

Eugene Onegin (Alexander Pushkin)

Letters

Dear Bunny, Dear Volodya:
The Nabokov–Wilson Letters, 1940–1971

Vladimir Nabokov: Selected Letters, 1940–1977

Miscellaneous

Poems and Problems

The Annotated Lolita

The Origin

(Dying

Vladimir

Edited

Alfred A. Kno

l of Lau

s Fun)

Nabokov

nitri Nabokov

ew York   2009

This Is a Borzoi Book
Published by Alfred A. Knopf

Copyright © 2009 by Dmitri Nabokov

All rights reserved. Published in the United States by Alfred A.
Knopf, a division of Random House, Inc., New York, and in Canada
by Random House of Canada Limited, Toronto.
www.aaknopf.com

Knopf, Borzoi Books, and the colophon are registered trademarks
of Random House, Inc.

This work includes previously unpublished material by Vladimir
Nabokov.

Library of Congress Cataloging-in-Publication Data

Nabokov, Vladimir Vladimirovich, 1899–1977.
The original of Laura (Dying is fun) / by Vladimir Nabokov ; edited
by Dmitri Nabokov.—1st ed.
        p.   cm.
    ISBN 978-0-307-27189-1 (alk. paper)
    I. Nabokov, Dmitri.   II. Title.
    PS3527.A15O75 2009
    813'.54—dc22
                    2009026357

Manufactured in China
First Edition

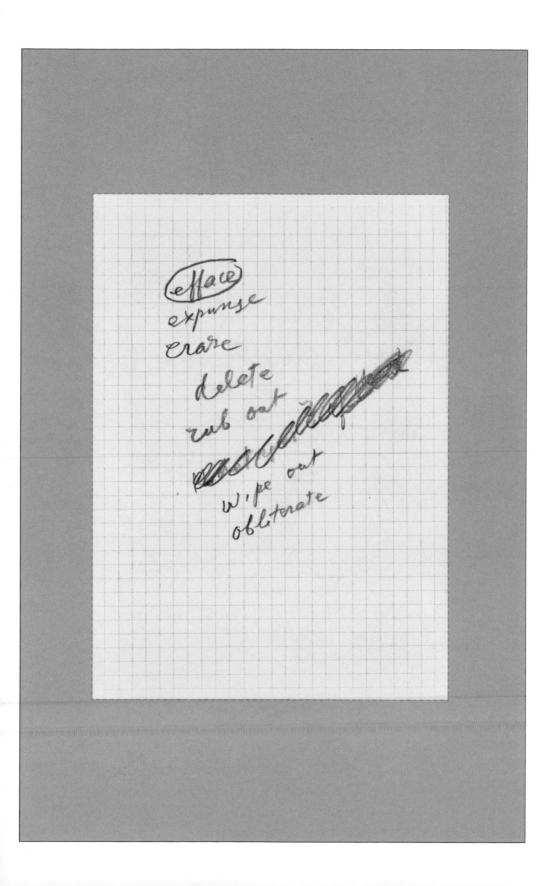

THE ORIGINAL OF LAURA

(*Dying Is Fun*)

VLADIMIR NABOKOV

Contents

Vladimir Nabokov

The Origin of Laura

Introduction

BY DMITRI NABOKOV

As a tepid spring settled on lakeside Switzerland in 1977, I was called from abroad to my father's bedside in a Lausanne clinic. During recovery from what is considered a banal operation, he had apparently been infected with a hospital bacillus that severely lessened his resistance. Such obvious signals of deterioration as dramatically reduced sodium and potassium levels had been totally ignored. It was high time to intervene if he was to be kept alive.

Transfer to the Vaud Cantonal University Hospital was immediately arranged, and a long and harrowing search for the noisome germ began.

My father had fallen on a hillside in Davos while pursuing his beloved pastime of entomology, and had gotten stuck in an awkward position on the steep slope as cabin-carloads of tourists responded with guffaws, misinterpreting as a holiday prank the cries for help and waves of a butterfly net. Officialdom can be ruthless; he was subsequently reprimanded by the hotel staff for stumbling back into the lobby, supported by two bellhops, with his shorts in disarray.

There may have been no connection, but this incident in 1975 seemed to set off a period of illness, which never quite receded until those dreadful days in Lausanne. There were several tentative forays to his former life at the *hôtel* Palace in Montreux, the majestic recollection of which floats forth as I read, in some asinine electronic biography, that the success of *Lolita* "did not go to Nabokov's head, and he continued to live in a *shabby Swiss hotel.*" (Italics mine.)

Nabokov did begin to lose his own physical majesty. His six-foot frame seemed to stoop a little, his steps on our lakeside promenades became short and insecure.

But he did not cease to write. He was working on a novel that he had begun in 1975—that same crucial year: an embryonic master-piece whose pockets of genius were beginning to pupate here and there on his ever-present index cards. He very seldom spoke about the details of what he was writing, but, perhaps because he felt that the opportunities of revealing them were numbered, he began to recount certain details to my mother and to me. Our after-dinner chats grew shorter and more fitful, and he would withdraw into his room as if in a hurry to complete his work.

Soon came the final ride to the Hôpital Nestlé. Father felt worse. The tests continued; a succession of doctors rubbed their chins as their bedside manner edged toward the graveside. Finally the draft from a window left open by a sneezing young nurse contributed to a terminal cold. My mother and I sat near him as, choking on the food I was urging him to consume, he succumbed, in three convulsive gasps, to congestive bronchitis.

Little was said about the exact causes of his malady. The death of the great man seemed to be veiled in embarrassed silence. Some years later, when, for biographical purposes, I wanted to pin things down, all access to the details of his death would remain obscure.

Only during the final stages of his life did I learn about certain confidential family matters. Among them were his express instruc-tions that the manuscript of *The Original of Laura* be destroyed if he were to die without completing it. Individuals of limited imagina-tion, intent on adding their suppositions to the maelstrom of hypotheses that has engulfed the unfinished work, have ridiculed the notion that a doomed artist might decide to destroy a work of his, whatever the reason, rather than allow it to outlive him.

An author may be seriously, even terminally ill and yet continue his desperate sprint against Fate to the last finish line, losing despite his intent to win. He may be thwarted by a chance occurrence or by the intervention of others, as was Nabokov many years earlier, on the way to the incinerator, when his wife snatched a draft of *Lolita* from his grasp.

- - - - - - - - - - - - - - - - -

My father's recollection and mine differed regarding the color of the impressive object that I, a child of almost six, distinguished with disbelief amid the puzzle-like jumble of buildings in the seaside town of Saint-Nazaire. It was the immense funnel of the *Champlain*, which was waiting to transport us to New York. I recall its being light yellow, while Father, in the concluding lines of *Speak, Memory*, says that it was white.

I shall stick to my image, no matter what researchers ferret from historical records of the French Line's liveries of the period. I am equally sure of the colors I saw in my final onboard dream as we approached America: the varying shades of depressing gray that colored my dream vision of a shabby, low-lying New York, instead of the exciting skyscrapers that my parents had been promising. Upon disembarking, we also saw two differing visions of America: a small flask of Cognac vanished from our baggage during the customs inspection; on the other hand, when my father (or was it my mother? memory sometimes conflates the two) attempted to pay the cabbie who took us to our destination with the entire contents of his wallet—a hundred-dollar bill of a currency that was new to us—the honest driver immediately refused the bill with a comprehending smile.

In the years that had preceded our departure from Europe, I had learned little, in a specific sense, of what my father "did." Even the term "writer" meant little to me. Only in the chance vignette that he might recount as a bedtime story might I retrospectively recognize the foretaste of a work that was in progress. The idea of a "book" was embodied by the many tomes bound in red leather that I would admire on the top shelves of the studies of my parents' friends. To me, they were "appetizing," as we would say in Russian. But my first "reading" was listening to my mother recite Father's Russian translation of *Alice in Wonderland*.

We traveled to the sunny beaches of the Riviera, and thus finally embarked for New York. There, after my first day at the now-defunct Walt Whitman School, I announced to my mother that I had learned English. I really learned English much more gradually, and it became my favorite and most flexible means of expression. I shall, however, always take pride in having been the only child in the world to have studied elementary Russian, with textbooks and all, under Vladimir Nabokov.

My father was in the midst of a transition of his own. Having grown up as a "perfectly normal trilingual child," he nonetheless found it profoundly challenging to abandon his "rich, untrammeled Russian" for a new language, not the domestic English he had shared with his Anglophone father, but an instrument as expressive, docile, and poetic as the mother tongue he had so thoroughly mastered. *The Real Life of Sebastian Knight*, his first English-language novel, cost him infinite doubt and suffering as he relinquished his beloved Russian—the "Softest of Tongues," as he entitled an English poem that appeared later (in 1947) in the *Atlantic Monthly*. Meanwhile, during the transition to a new tongue and on the verge of our move to America, he had written his last significant freestanding prose work in Russian (in other words, neither a portion of a work in progress nor a Russian version of an existing one). This was *Volshebnik* (*The Enchanter*), in a sense a precursor of *Lolita*. He thought he had destroyed or lost this small manuscript and that its creative essence had been consumed by *Lolita*. He recalled having read it to group of friends one Paris night, blue-papered against the threat of Nazi bombs. When, eventually, it did turn up again, he examined it with his wife, and they decided, in 1959, that it would make artistic sense if it were "done into English by the Nabokovs" and published.

That was not accomplished until a decade after his death, and the publication of *Lolita* itself preceded that of its forebear. Several American publishers, fearing the repercussions of the delicate subject matter of *Lolita,* had abstained. Convinced that it would remain forever a victim of incomprehension, Nabokov had resolved to destroy the draft, and it was only the intervention of Véra Nabokov that, on two occasions, kept it from going up in smoke in our Ithaca incinerator.

Eventually, unaware of the publisher's dubious reputation, Nabokov consented to have an agent place it with Girodias's Olympia Press. And it was the eulogy of Graham Greene that propelled *Lolita* far beyond the trashy tropics of Cancer and Capricorn, inherited by Girodias from his father at Obelisk, and along with pornier Olympia stablemates, on its way to becoming what some have acclaimed as one of the best books ever written.

The highways and motels of 1940s America are immortalized in this proto–road novel, and countless names and places live on in Nabokov's puns and anagrams. In 1961 the Nabokovs would take up residence at the Montreux Palace and there, on one of their first evenings, a well-meaning maid would empty forever a butterfly-adorned gift wastebasket of its contents: a thick batch of U.S. road maps on which my father had meticulously marked the roads and towns that he and my mother had traversed. Chance comments of his were recorded there, as well as names of butterflies and their habitats. How sad, especially now when every such detail is being researched by scholars on several continents. How sad, too, that a first edition of *Lolita,* lovingly inscribed to me, was purloined from a New York cellar and, on its way to the digs of a Cornell graduate student, sold for two dollars.

The theme of book burning would pursue us. Invited to lecture at Harvard on *Don Quixote,* Nabokov, while recognizing certain merits of Cervantes, criticized the book as "crude" and "cruel." The expression "torn apart," applied years later to Nabokov's evaluation, was further garbled by half-literate journalists until one perceived the image of a caricature Nabokov holding up a blazing volume before his class, accompanied by all the appropriate de rigueur moralizing.

And so, at last, we come to *Laura,* and again to thoughts of fire. During the last months of his life in the Lausanne hospital, Nabokov was working feverishly on the book, impervious to hoaxes from the insensitive, quizzes from the well-meaning, conjectures from the curious in the outside world, and to his own suffering. Among those were incessant inflammations under and around his toenails. At times, he felt almost as if he would rather be rid of them altogether than undergo tentative pedicures from the nurses, and the compulsion to correct them and seek relief by painfully digging at the digits himself. We shall recognize, in *Laura,* some echoes of these torments.

He looked at the sunny outdoors and softly exclaimed that a certain butterfly was already on the wing. But there were to be no more rambles on the hillside meadows, net in hand, book working in his mind. The book worked on, but in the claustrophobic microcosm of a hospital room, and Nabokov began to fear that his inspiration and his concentration would not win the race against his failing health. He then had a very serious conversation with his wife, in which he impressed upon her that if *Laura* remained unfinished at his death, it was to be burned.

The lesser minds among the hordes of letter writers that were to descend upon me would affirm that if an artist wishes to destroy a work of his that he has deemed imperfect or incomplete, he should logically proceed to do so neatly and providently ahead of time. These sages forget, though, that Nabokov did *not* desire to burn *The Original of Laura* willy-nilly, but to live on for the last few card lengths needed to finish at least a complete draft. It was also theorized that Franz Kafka had deliberately charged Max Brod with the destruction of the reprinted *Metamorphosis* and other masterpieces published and unpublished, including *The Castle* and *The Trial,* knowing full well that Brod could never bring himself to carry out the task (a rather naive stratagem for a brave and lucid mind like Kafka's), and that Nabokov had exercised similar reasoning when he assigned *Laura's* annihilation to my mother, who was an impeccably courageous and trustworthy emissary. Her failure to perform was rooted in procrastination—procrastination due to age, weakness, and immeasurable love.

For my part, when the task passed to me, I did a great deal of thinking. I have said and written more than once that, to me, my parents, in a sense, had never died but lived on, looking over my shoulder in a kind of virtual limbo, available to offer a thought or counsel to assist me with a vital decision, whether a crucial mot juste or a more mundane concern. I did not need to borrow my "*ton bon*" (thus deliberately garbled) from the titles of fashionable morons but had it from the source. If it pleases an adventurous commentator to liken the case to mystical phenomena, so be it. I decided at this juncture that, in putative retrospect, Nabokov would not have wanted me to become his Person from Porlock or allow little Juanita Dark—for that was the name of an early Lolita, destined for cremation—to burn like a latter-day Jeanne d'Arc.

On Father's ever shorter and less frequent visits home we tried bravely to keep up our chatty dinnertime conversation, but the otherworldly world of *Laura* would not be mentioned. By that time I and, I think, my mother knew, in every sense, how things would go.

Some time passed before I could bring myself to open Father's index-card box. I needed to traverse a stifling barrier of pain before touching the cards he had lovingly arranged and shuffled. After several tries, during a hospital stay of my own, I first read what, despite its incompleteness, was unprecedented in structure and style, written in a new "softest of tongues" that English had become for Nabokov. I attacked the task of ordering and preparing, and then dictating, a preliminary transcript to my faithful secretary Cristiane Galliker. *Laura* lived on in a penumbra, emerging only occasionally for my perusal and the bits of editing I dared perform. Very gradually I became accustomed to this disturbing specter that seemed to be living a simultaneous twin life of its own in the stillness of a strongbox and the meanders of my mind. I could no longer even think of burning *Laura,* and my urge was to let it peek for an occasional instant from its gloom. Hence my minimal mentions of the work, which I sensed my father would not disapprove, and which, together with a few approximate leaks and suppositions from others, led to the fragmentary notions of *Laura* now flaunted by a press ever eager for the tasty scoop. Nor, as I have said, do I think that my father or my father's shade would have opposed the release of *Laura* once *Laura* had survived the hum of time this long. A survival to which I may have contributed, motivated not by playfulness or calculation, but by an otherforce I could not resist. Should I be damned or thanked?

But why, Mr. Nabokov, why did you *really* decide to publish *Laura*?

Well, I am a nice guy, and, having noticed that people the world over find themselves on a first-name basis with me as they empathize with "Dmitri's dilemma," I felt it would be kind to alleviate their sufferings.

Acknowledgments

For their generous assistance and advice:
Professor Gennady Barabtarlo
Professor Brian Boyd
Ariane Csonka Comstock
Aleksei Konovalov
Professor Stanislav Shvabrin
Ron Rosenbaum, who could not have set off a better publicity campaign had it been planned (it was not).

To all the worldwide contributors of opinion, comment, and advice, of whatever its stripe, who imagined that their views, sometimes deftly expressed, might somehow change mine.

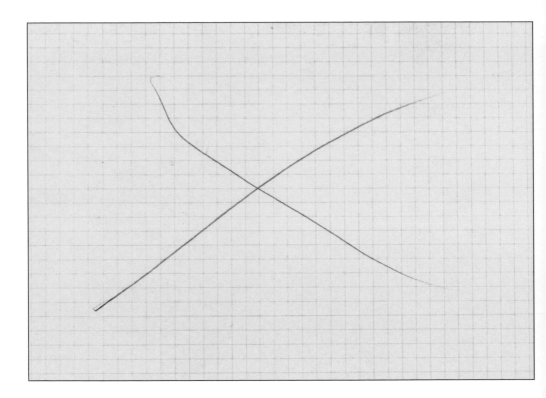

A Note on the Text

The typeset text of *The Original of Laura* preserves Vladimir Nabokov's original markings from the handwritten cards. Nonstandard spellings (i.e., "bycycle") and punctuation have been retained, and accents have not been added to French words where they do not appear on the cards. Some additional material is included within brackets or as footnotes for clarity.

The photos of the cards that accompany the text are perforated and can be removed and rearranged, as the author likely did when he was writing the novel.

Vladimir Nabokov

The Original of Laura

Vladimir Nabokov

The Original of Laura

The Original of Laura

Ch. One

Her husband, she answered, was a writer, too—at least, after a fashion. Fat men beat their wives, it is said, and he certainly looked fierce, when he caught her riffling through his papers. He pretended to slam down a marble paperweight and crush this weak little hand (displaying the little hand in febrile motion) Actually she was searching for a silly business letter—and not in the least trying to decipher his mysterious

- - - - - - - - - - - - - - - - - -

manuscript. Oh no, it was not a work of fiction which
one dashes off, you know, to make
money; it was a mad neurologist's
testament, a
kind of Poisonous Opus as in that film.
It had cost him,
and would still
cost him, years of toil, but the thing
was, of course, an absolute
secret. If she mentioned it at all she
added, it was because she was drunk.
She wished to be taken home or preferably
to some cool quiet place with a clean bed
and room service. She wore a strapless gown

2

---

manuscript. Oh no, it was not a work of fiction which one
dashes off, you know, to make money; it was a mad neurologist's testament, a kind of Poisonous Opus as in that film.
It had cost him, and would still cost him, years of toil, but
the thing was of course, an absolute secret. If she mentioned it at all, she added, it was because she was drunk.
She wished to be taken home or preferably to some cool
quiet place with a clean bed and room service. She wore a
strapless gown

----

and slippers of black velvet. Her bare insteps
were as white as her young shoulders. The
party seemed to have degenerated into
a lot of sober eyes staring at her with
nasty compassion from every corner,
every cushion and ashtray, and even
from the hills of the ~~night the~~
~~past~~ spring night framed in the
open french window. Mrs. Carr, her
hostess, repeated what a pity it was
that Philip could not come or rather
that Flora could not have induced

3

---

and slippers of black velvet. Her bare insteps were as white
as her young shoulders. The party seemed to have degenerated into a lot of sober eyes staring at her with nasty compassion from every corner, every cushion and ashtray, and
even from the hills of the spring night framed in the open
french window. Mrs. Carr, her hostess, repeated what a pity
it was that Philip could not come or rather that Flora could
not have induced

him to come! I'll drug him ~~and~~
~~again~~ next time said Flora,

~~idebody Flora ace nypor~~
~~acajoule~~ rummaging all around
her seat for her small formless vanity
bag, a blind black puppy. Here it is,
cried an anonymous girl, squatting
quickly.

   Mrs Carr's nephew, Anthony Carr,
and his wife Winny, ~~were~~ ~~innocent~~ one of those,
~~innocent~~ easy going, over-generous
couples that positively crave to
lend their flat to a friend, any friend, when
they ~~and their two~~ dog do not happen

him to come! I'll drug him next time said Flora, rummaging
all around her seat for her small formless vanity bag, a blind
black puppy. Here it is, cried an anonymous girl, squatting
quickly.

   Mrs Carr's nephew, Anthony Carr, and his wife Winny,
were one of those easygoing, over-generous couples that
positively crave to lend their flat to a friend, any friend,
when they and their dog do not happen

----

to need it. Flora spotted at once ~~the~~
~~the~~ alien creams in the bathroom and the
open can of Fido's Feast next to the~~re~~
~~naked cheese~~ in the cluttered fridge
A brief set of instructions (~~meaning~~
~~#~~ (pertaining to the superintendent and the charwoman
~~wring~~) ended on: "Ring up my aunt Emily Carr"
which evidently had be already done
to lamentation in Heaven and laughter
in Hell. The double bed was made
but was unfresh inside. With
comic fastidiousness Flora spread

5
_____

to need it. Flora spotted at once the alien creams in the
bathroom and the open can of Fido's Feast next to the naked
cheese in the cluttered fridge. A brief set of instructions
(pertaining to the superintend[e]nt and the charwoman)
ended on: "Ring up my aunt Emily Carr," which evidently
had be[en] already done to lamentation in Heaven and
laughter in Hell. The double bed was made but was unfresh
inside. With comic fastidiousness Flora spread

----

her fur coat over it ~~before undressing~~
before undressing and lying down.
Then Where was the damned valise
that has been brought up earlier? ~~~~
In the vestibule closet. Had everything
to be shaken out before the pair
of morocco slippers could be located
infoetally folded in their zippered
pouch? ~~Hiding under the~~
shaving kit. All the towels in the
bathroom, ~~whether pink or green, were~~
of a thick, soggy-looking, ~~spongy-like~~ texture.

6

---

her fur coat over it before undressing and lying down.

Where was the damned valise that had been brought up earlier? In the vestibule closet. Had everything to be shaken out before the pair of morocco slippers could be located foetally folded in their zippered pouch? Hiding under the shaving kit. All the towels in the bathroom, whether pink or green, were of a thick, soggy-looking, spongy-like texture.

- - - - - - - - - - - - - - - - - -

copy out again

Let us choose the smallest. On the way back
the distal edge of the right slipper lost
its grip and had to be pried at the grateful heel
with a finger for shoeing-horn.
no quotes ¶ Oh, hurry up, she said softly
no comma ¶ That first surrender of hers
was a little sudden, if not down.right
unnerving. A pause for some light
caresses, concealed embarrassment,
feigned amusement, prefactory contemplation

~~scribbled out~~ She was ~~an~~

7

Let us choose the smallest. On the way back the distal edge
of the right slipper lost its grip and had to be pried at the
grateful heel with a finger for shoeing-horn.

Oh hurry up, she said softly[.]

That first surrender of hers was a little sudden, if not
downright unnerving. A pause for some light caresses,
concealed embarrassment, feigned amusement, prefactory
contemplation[.] She was

----

an extravagantly slender girl. Her ribs showed. The conspicuous knobs of her hipbones framed a hollowed abdomen, so flat as to belie the notion of « belly » Her exquisite bone structure immediately slipped into a novel — became in fact the secret structure of that novel, besides supporting a number of poems. The cup-sized breasts of that twenty-four years old impatient beauty seemed a dozen years younger than she, with those pale squinty nipples and firm form.

8

---

an extravagantly slender girl. Her ribs showed. The conspicuous knobs of her hipbones framed a hollowed abdomen, so flat as to belie the notion of "belly". Her exquisite bone structure immediately slipped into a novel—became in fact the secret structure of that novel, besides supporting a number of poems. The cup-sized breasts of that twenty-four year old impatient beauty seemed a dozen years younger than she, with those pale squinty nipples and firm form.

- - - - - - - - - - - - - - - - - -

Her painted eyelids were closed. A tear of no particular meaning ~~gemmed~~ gemmed the hard top of her cheek. Nobody could tell what went on in that little head. Waves of desire rippled there, a recent lover fell back in a swoon, hygienic doubts were raised and dismissed, contempt for everyone but herself advertised with a flush of warmth its constant presence, here it is, cried what's her name squatting quickly, my darling, dushka moya (eyebrows

9

Her painted eyelids were closed. A tear of no particular meaning gemmed the hard top of her cheek. Nobody could tell what went on in that little head[.] Waves of desire rippled there, a recent lover fell back in a swoon, hygienic doubts were raised and dismissed, contempt for everyone but herself advertised with a flush of warmth its constant presence, here it is, cried what's her name squatting quickly. My darling, dushka moya (eyebrows

----

went up, eyes opened and closed again, she didn't meet Russians often, this should be pondered)

¶ Masking her face, coating her side, pinaforing her stomach with kisses — all very acceptable while they remained dry.

¶ Her frail, docile frame when turned over by hand revealed new marvels — the mobile omoplates of a child being tubbed, the incurvation of a ballerina's spine, narrow nates

10

went up, eyes opened and closed again, she didnt meet Russians often, this should be pondered.)

Masking her face, coating her side, pinaforing her stomack with kisses—all very acceptable while they remained dry.

Her frail, docile frame when turned over by hand revealed new marvels—the mobile omoplates of a child being tubbed, the incurvation of a ballerina's spine, narrow nates

of an ambiguous irresistable charm (nature's beastliest bluff, said Paul de G watching a dour old don watching ~~&~~ boys & bathing)

    Only by identifying her with an unwritten, half-written, rewritten difficult book could one hope to render at last what ~~[illegible]~~

~~[crossed out]~~

11

---

of an ambiguous irresistable charm (nature's beastliest bluff, said Paul de G watching a dour old don watching boys bathing)

    Only by identifying her with an unwritten, half-written, rewritten difficult book could one hope to render at last what

- - - - - - - - - - - - - - - - - -

contemporary descriptions of intercourse
so seldom convey, because newborn and
thus generalized, in the sense of primitive
organisms of art as opposed to
the personal achievement of great
English poets dealing with
an evening in the country, a bit of
sky in a river, the nostalgia of
remote sounds — things utterly beyond the
(reach) of Homer or Horace. Readers are
directed to that book — on a very
high shelf, in a very bad light — but

12

---

contemporary descriptions of intercourse so seldom convey, because newborn and thus generalized, in the sense of primitive organisms of art as opposed to the personal achievement of great English poets dealing with an evening in the country, a bit of sky in a river, the nostalgia of remote sounds—things utterly beyond the reach of Homer or Horace. Readers are directed to that book—on a very high shelf, in a very bad light—but

----

already existing, as magic exists, and death, and as shall exist, from now on, the mouth she made automatically while using ~~tattad~~ that towel to wipe her thighs after the promised withdrawal.

¶ ~~A copy of~~ Glist's dreadful "Glandscape" ~~(receding ovals)~~ adorned the wall. Vital and serene, according to philistine Flora ~~Atho~~ Auroral rumbles and bangs had begun jolting the cold misty city

¶ She consulted the ~~onyx eye~~ on her wrist. It was too tiny and not

---

13

already existing, as magic exists, and death, and as shall exist, from now on, the mouth she made automatically while using that towel to wipe her thighs after the promised withdrawal.

A copy of Glist's dreadful "Glandscape" (receding ovals) adorned the wall. Vital and serene, according to philistine Flora. Auroral rumbles and bangs had begun jolting the cold misty city[.]

She consulted the onyx eye on her wrist. It was too tiny and not

costly enough for its size to go right,
she said (translating from Russian)
and it was the first time in her stormy
life that she knew anyone take of his
watch to make love. But I'm sure
it is sufficiently late to ring up another
fellow (stretching her swift cruel
arm toward the bedside telephone.)"
    She who mislaid everything dialled
fluently a long number
            " you were asleep? I've
shattered your sleep? That's what you

14

costly enough for its size to go right, she said (translating
from Russian) and it was the first time in her stormy life
that she knew anyone take of[f] his watch to make love. "But
I'm sure it is sufficiently late to ring up another fellow
(stretching her swift cruel arm toward the bedside telephone)."

She who mislaid everything dialled fluently a long
number

"You were asleep? I've shattered your sleep? That's what
you

----

deserve. Now listen carefully." And
with tigerish zest, monstrously magnifying
a trivial tiff she had had with
him whose pyjamas (the idiot
subject of the tiff) were changing
the while, in the spectrum of his
surprise and distress, from heliotrope
to a sickly gray, she dismissed
the poor oaf for ever.
    "That's done, she said, resolutely
for replacing the receiver. Was I game now
another round, she wanted to know.

---

deserve. Now listen carefully." And with tigerish zest, monstrously magnifying a trivial tiff she had had with him whose pyjamas (the idiot subject of the tiff) were changing the while, in the spectrum of his surprise and distress, from heliotrope to a sickly gray, she dismissed the poor oaf for ever.

"That's done,["] she said, resolutely replacing the receiver. Was I game now for another round, she wanted to know.

No? Not even a quickie? Well, tant pis.
Try to find me some liquor in their kitchen,
and then take me home.
¶ The position of her head, its trustful
poximity, its gratefully shouldered
weight, the tickle of her hair, endured
all through the drive; yet ~~too much~~
~~complain~~ she was not asleep
and with the greatest exactitude had
the taxi stop to let her out ~~corner~~
~~corner~~ at the corner of Heine street,
not too far from, nor too close to, her

16

No? Not even a quickie? Well, tant pis. Try to find me some
liquor in their kitchen, and then take me home.

The position of her head, its trustful poximity, its gratefully shouldered weight, the tickle of her hair, endured all
through the drive; yet she was not asleep and with the
greatest exactitude had the taxi stop to let her out at the
corner of Heine street, not too far from, nor too close to,
her

- - - - - - - - - - - - - - - - - -

house. This was an old villa backed by tall trees. In the shadows of a side alley a young man with a mackintosh over his white pyjamas was wringing his hands. The street lights were going out in alternate order, the odd numbers first. Along the pavement in front of the villa her obese husband, in a rumpled black suit and tartan booties with clasps, was walking a striped cat on an overlong leash. She made for the front door.

17

---

house. This was an old villa backed by tall trees. In the shadows of a side alley a young man with a mackintosh over his white pyjamas was wringing his hands. The street lights were going out in alternate order, the odd numbers first. Along the pavement in front of the villa her obese husband, in a rumpled black suit and tartan booties with clasps, was walking a striped cat on an overlong leash. She made for the front door.

Her husband followed, now carrying the
cat. The scene might be called somewhat
incongrous. The animal seemed naively
fascinated by the snake trailing
behind on the ground.
¶¶ Not wishing to harness herself
to futurity, she declined to discuss another
rendez-vous. To prod her slightly, a
messenger called at her domicile three days
later. He brought from the favorite
florist of fashionable girls a banal
bevy ~~crossed out~~

18

Her husband followed, now carrying the cat. The scene might be called somewhat incongr[u]ous. The animal seemed naively fascinated by the snake trailing behind on the ground.

Not wishing to harness herself to futurity, she declined to discuss another rendez-vous. To prod her slightly, a messenger called at her domicile three days later[.] He brought from the favorite florist of fashionable girls a banal bevy

----

of bird-of-paradise flowers. Cora, the
mulatto chamber maid, who let him in,
surveyed the shabby courier, his comic
cap, his wan countenance with it
three days growth of blond beard, and
was about to ᵃⁱˢᵉ ʰᵉʳ ᶜʰⁱⁿ ᵃⁿᵈ embrace his rustling
load but he said "No, I've been
ordered to give this to Madame
herself" "You French?", asked
scornful Cora (the whole scene was
pretty artificial in a fishy theatrical
way). He shook his head — and here

19

---

of bird-of-paradise flowers. Cora, the mulatto chamber-
maid, who let him in, surveyed the shabby courier, his
comic cap, his wan countenance with it[s] three days
growth of blond beard, and was about to raise her chin and
embrace his rustling load but he said "No, I've been
ordered to give this to Madame herself". "You French?",
asked scornful Cora (the whole scene was pretty artificial in
a fishy theatrical way). He shook his head—and here

- - - - - - - - - - - - - - - - - -

Madame appeared from the breakfast room. First of all she dismissed Cora with the strelitzias (hateful blooms, regalized bananas, really).

¶ "Look," she said to the beaming bum, "if you ever repeat this idiotic performance, I will never see you again. I swear I won't! In fact, I have a great mind —" He flattened her against the wall between his outstretched arms; Flora ducked, and freed herself, and showed him the door; but the telephone was already ringing ~~certainly~~ ecstatically when he reached his lodgings.

—.—

20

Madame appeared from the breakfast room. First of all she dismissed Cora with the strelitzias (hateful blooms, regalized bananas, really).

"Look," she said to the beaming bum, "if you ever repeat this idiotic performance, I will never see you again. I swear I won't! In fact, I have a great mind—" He flattened her against the wall between his outstretched arms; Flora ducked, and freed herself, and showed him the door; but the telephone was already ringing ecstatically when he reached his lodgings.

Ch. Two

Her grandfather, the painter Lev Linde, emigrated in 1920 from Moscow to New York with his wife Eva and his son Adam. He also brought over a large collection of his landscapes, either unsold or loaned to him by kind friends and ignorant institutions — pictures that were said to be the glory of Russia, the pride of the people. How many times art albums had reproduced those meticulous masterpieces — clearings in pine woods, with a bear cub or two, and brown brooks between thawing snow-banks, and the vastness of purple heaths!

Two 1

Ch. Two

Her grandfather, the painter Lev Linde, emigrated in 1920 from Moscow to New York with his wife Eva and his son Adam. He also brought over a large collection of his landscapes, either unsold or loaned to him by kind friends and ignorant institutions—pictures that were said to be the glory of Russia, the pride of the people. How many times art albums had reproduced those meticulous masterpieces— clearings in pine woods, with a bear cub or two, and brown brooks between thawing snow-banks, and the vastness of purple heaths!

Native "decadents" had been calling them "calendar tripe" for the last three decades; yet *Linde* had always had an army of stout admirers; mighty few of them turned up at his exhibitions in America. Very soon a number of unconsolable oils found themselves being shipped back to Moscow, while another batch moped in rented flats before trouping up to the attic or creeping down to the marketstall.

¶ What can be sadder than a discouraged

Two 2

Native "decadents" had been calling them "calendar tripe" for the last three decades; yet Linde had always had an army of stout admirers; mighty few of them turned up at his exhibitions in America. Very soon a number of unconsolable oils found themselves being shipped back to Moscow, while another batch moped in rented flats before trouping up to the attic or creeping down to the marketstall.

What can be sadder than a discouraged

----

artist dying not from his own commonplace maladies, but from the cancer of oblivion invading his once famous "pictures such as "April in Yalta" or "The Old Bridge? Let us not dwell on the the choice of the wrong place of exile. Let us not linger at that pityful bedside. ¶ His son Adam Lind (he dropped the last letter on the tacite advice of a misprint in a catalogue) was more successful. By the age of thirty he was, he had become a fashionable photographer. He married the ballerina Lanskaya,

Two 3

artist dying not from his own commonplace maladies, but from the cancer of oblivion invading his once famous pictures such as "April in Yalta" or "The Old Bridge["]? Let us not dwell on the choice of the wrong place of exile. Let us not linger at that pityful bedside.

His son Adam Lind (he dropped the last letter on the tacite advice of a misprint in a catalogue) was more successful. By the age of thirty he had become a fashionable photographer. He married the ballerina Lanskaya,

----

a delightful dancer, though with something fragile and gauche about her that kept her teetering on a narrow ledge beetween benevolent recognition and the rave reviews of nonentities. Her first lovers belonged mostly to the Union of Property Movers, simple fellows of Polish extraction; but Flora was probably Adam's daughter. Three years after her birth Adam discovered that the boy he loved had strangled another, unattainable, boy

Two 4

a delightful dancer, though with something fragile and gauche about her that kept her teetering on a narrow ledge between benevolent recognition and the rave reviews of nonentities. Her first lovers belonged mostly to the Union of Property Movers, simple fellows of Polish extraction; but Flora was probably Adam's daughter. Three years after her birth Adam discovered that the boy he loved had strangled another, unattainable, boy

whom he loved even more. Adam Lind had always had an inclination for trick photography and this time, before shooting himself in a Montecarlo hotel (on the night, sad to relate, of his wife's very real success in Piker's "Narcisse et Narcette"), he geared and focussed his camera in a corner of the drawing room so as to record the event from different angles. These automatic pictures of his last moments and of a table's lion-paws did not come out to well; but his widow

Two 5

whom he loved even more. Adam Lind had always had an inclination for trick photography and this time, before shooting himself in a Montecarlo hotel (on the night, sad to relate, of his wife's very real success in Piker's "Narcisse et Narcette"), he geared and focussed his camera in a corner of the drawing room so as to record the event from different angles. These automatic pictures of his last moments and of a table's lion-paws did not come out to[o] well; but his widow

easily sold them for the price of a flat in Paris to the local magazine <u>Pitch</u> which specialized in soccer and diabolical <u>faits-divers</u>.

With her little daughter, an English governess, a Russian nanny, and a cosmopolitan lover, she settled in Paris, then moved to Florence, sojourned in London and returned to France. Her art was not strong enough to survive the loss of good looks as well as a certain worsening flaw in her pretty but too prominent right omoplate, and by the

---

Two 6

---

easily sold them for the price of a flat in Paris to the local magazine <u>Pitch</u> which specialized in soccer and diabolical <u>faits-divers</u>.

With her little daughter, an English governess, a Russian nanny, and a cosmopolitan lover, she settled in Paris, then moved to Florence, sojourned in London and returned to France. Her art was not strong enough to survive the loss of good looks as well as a certain worsening flaw in her pretty but too prominent right omoplate, and by the

----

age of forty or so we find her reduced to giving
dancing lessons at a not quite first-rate
school in Paris.

¶ Her glamorous ~~lovers~~ were now replaced
by an elderly but still vigorous Englishmen
~~Englishmen~~ who sought abroad a refuge
from taxes and ^a^ convenient place to conduct
his not quite legal transactions in the
traffic of wines. He was what used to
be termed a <u>charmeur</u>. His name,
~~no doubt~~ assumed, was Hubert H. Hubert.
¶ Flora, a lovely child, as she said

Two 7

age of forty or so we find her reduced to giving dancing
lessons at a not quite first-rate school in Paris.

Her glamorous lovers were now replaced by an elderly
but still vigorous Englishm[a]n who sought abroad a refuge
from taxes and a convenient place to conduct his not quite
legal transactions in the traffic of wines. He was what used
to be termed a <u>charmeur</u>. His name, no doubt assumed, was
Hubert H. Hubert.

Flora, a lovely child, as she said

----

herself with a slight shake (dreamy? ~~incredulous~~ Incredulous?) of her head ~~every~~ time she spoke of those prepubescent years, had a gray home life marred by ill health, ~~boredom~~ and boredom. Only some very expensive, super-Oriental doctor with long gentle fingers could have analyzed her nightly dreams of erotic torture in so called "labs", major and minor laboratories with red curtains. She did not remember her father and rather disliked her mother. She was often alone in

---

Two 8

---

herself with a slight shake (dreamy? Incredulous?) of her head every time she spoke of those prepubescent years, had a gray home life marked by ill health, and boredom. Only some very expensive, super-Oriental doctor with long gentle fingers could have analyzed her nightly dreams of erotic torture in so called "labs", major and minor laboratories with red curtains. She did not remember her father and rather disliked her mother. She was often alone in

----

the house with Mr. Hubert, who constantly "prowled" (rodait) around her, humming a monotonous tune and sort of mesmerising her, envelopping her, so to speak in some sticky invisible substance and coming closer and closer no matter what way she turned. For instance she did not dare to let her arms hang aimlessly lest her knuckles came into contact with some horrible part of that kindly but smelly and "pushing" old male.

Two 9

----

the house with Mr. Hubert, who constantly "prowled" (<u>rodait</u>) around her, humming a monotonous tune and sort of mesmerising her, envelopping her, so to speak in some sticky invisible substance and coming closer and closer no matter what way she turned. For instance she did not dare to let her arms hang aimlessly lest her knuckles came into contact with some horrible part of that kindly but smelly and "pushing" old male.

(her)

He told stories about his sad life, he told her about his daughter who was just like her, same age—twelve—, same eyelashes—darker than the dark blue of the iris, same hair, blondish or rather palomino, and so silky—if he could be allowed to stroke it, or l'effleurer des levres, like this, thats all, thank you. Poor Daisy had been crushed to death by a backing lorry on a country road —short cut home from school —

Two 10

He told her stories about his sad life, he told her about his daughter who was just like her, same age—twelve—, same eyelashes—darker than the dark blue of the iris, same hair, blondish or rather palomino, and so silky—if he could be allowed to stroke it, or l'effleurer des levres, like this, thats all, thank you. Poor Daisy had been crushed to death by a backing lorry on a country road—short cut home from school—

through a muddy construction site — abominable
tragedy — her mother died of a broken heart.
Mr Hubert sat on Flora's bed and nodded
his bald head acknow-
ledging all the offences of life, and
wiped his eyes with a violet
handkerchief which turned orange — a
little parlor trick — when he stuffed it back
into his heart-pocket, and continued to
nod as he tried to adjust
his thick outsole to a pattern of
the carpet. He looked now like a
not too successful conjuror paid to tell

Two 11

---

through a muddy construction site—abominable tragedy—her mother died of a broken heart. Mr Hubert sat on Flora's bed and nodded his bald head acknowledging all the offences of life, and wiped his eyes with a violet handkerchief which turned orange—a little parlor trick—when he stuffed it back into his heart-pocket, and continued to nod as he tried to adjust his thick outsole to a pattern of the carpet. He looked now like a not too successful conjuror paid to tell

fairytales to a sleepy child at bedtime, but he sat a little too close. Flora wore a nightgown with short sleeves copied from that of the Montglas de Sancerre girl, ~~hard~~ a very ~~sweets~~ and depraved schoolmate, who taught her where to kick an enterprising gentleman.

A week or so later Flora happened to be laid up with a chest cold. The mercury went up to 38° in the late afternoon and she complained of a dull buzz

---

Two 12

---

fairytales to a sleepy child at bedtime, but he sat a little too close. Flora wore a nightgown with short sleeves copied from that of the Montglas de Sancerre girl, a very sweet and depraved schoolmate, who taught her where to kick an enterprising gentleman.

    A week or so later Flora happened to be laid up with a chest cold. The mercury went up to 38° in the late afternoon and she complained of a dull buzz

- - - - - - - - - - - - - - - - - -

in the temples. Mrs Lind cursed the old housemaid for buying asparagus instead of Asperin and hurried to the pharmacy herself. Mr Hubert had brought his pet a thoughtful present: a miniature chess set ("she knew the moves") with tickly-looking little holes bored in the squares to admit and grip the red and white pieces; the pin-sized pawns penetrated easily, but the slightly larger noblemen had to be forced in with an ennervating joggle. The pharmacy was perhaps closed

Two 13

---

in the temples. Mrs Lind cursed the old housemaid for buying asparagus instead of Asperin and hurried to the pharmacy herself. Mr Hubert had brought his pet a thoughtful present: a miniature chess set ("she knew the moves") with tickly-looking little holes bored in the squares to admit and grip the red and white pieces; the pin-sized pawns penetrated easily, but the slightly larger noblemen had to be forced in with an ennervating joggle. The pharmacy was perhaps closed

----

and she had to go to the one next to the church
or else she had met some friend of hers
in the street and would never return. A
fourfold smell — tobacco, sweat, rum
and bad teeth — emanated from poor
old harmless Mr Hubert, it was
all very pathetic. His fat porous nose with
red nostrils full of hair nearly touched her
bare throat as he helped to prop the
pillows behind her shoulders, and the muddy road
was again, was for ever a short cut between
here and school, between school and death,

Two 14

----

and she had to go to the one next to the church or else she
had met some friend of hers in the street and would never
return. A fourfold smell—tobacco, sweat, rum and bad
teeth—emanated from poor old harmless Mr Hubert, it was
all very pathetic. His fat porous nose with red nostrils full of
hair nearly touched her bare throat as he helped to prop the
pillows behind her shoulders, and the muddy road was
again, was for ever a short cut between her and school,
between school and death,

----

with Daisy's bycycle wobbling in the
indelible fog. She, too, had " known
the moves", and had loved the en passant
trick as one loves a new toy, but it
cropped up so seldom, though he tried
to prepare those magic positions where the
ghost of a pawn can be captured on the square
it has crossed. ~~~~~~~~~~~~~~~~~~~~~~
~~~~~~~~~ Fever, however, turns games of
skill into the stuff of nightmares. After
a few minutes of play Flora grew tired
of it, put a rook in her mouth, ejected it,

Two 15

---

with Daisy's bycycle wobbling in the indelible fog. She, too,
had "known the moves", and had loved the <u>en passant</u> trick
as one loves a new toy, but it cropped up so seldom, though
he tried to prepare those magic positions where the ghost of
a pawn can be captured on the square it has crossed.

    Fever, however, turns games of skill into the stuff of
nightmares. After a few minutes of play Flora grew tired
of it, put a rook in her mouth, ejected it,

----

clowning dully. She pushed the board away and Mr. Hubert carefully removed it to the chair that supported the tea things. Then, with a father's sudden concern, he said "I'm afraid you are chilly, my love," and plunging a hand under the bedclothes from his vantage point at the footboard, he felt her shins Flora uttered a yelp and then a few screams. Freeing themselves from the tumbled sheets her pedalling legs hit him in the crotch. As he lurched aside, the teapot, a saucer of raspberry jam,

Two 16

---

clowning dully. She pushed the board away and Mr. Hubert carefully removed it to the chair that supported the tea things. Then, with a father's sudden concern, he said "I'm afraid you are chilly, my love," and plunging a hand under the bedclothes from his vantage point at the footboard, he felt her shins[.] Flora uttered a yelp and then a few screams. Freeing themselves from the tumbled sheets her pedalling legs hit him in the crotch. As he lurched aside, the teapot, a saucer of raspberry jam,

an several tiny chessmen joined in the silly fray. Mrs Lind who had just returned and was sampling some grapes she had bought, heard the screams and the crash and arrived at a dancer's run. She soothed the absolutely furious, deeply insulted Mr Hubert before scolding her daughter. He was a dear man, and his life lay in ruins all around him. He wanted to marry him, saying she was the image of the young actress who had been his wife, and indeed to judge by the photographs

Two 17

an[d] several tiny chessmen joined in the silly fray. Mrs Lind who had just returned and was sampling some grapes she had bought, heard the screams and the crash and arrived at a dancer's run. She soothed the absolutely furious, deeply insulted Mr Hubert before scolding her daughter. He was a dear man, and his life lay in ruins all around him. He wanted [her] to marry him, saying she was the image of the young actress who had been his wife, and indeed to judge by the photographs

she, Madame Lanskaya, did ressemble ~~poor Daisy's mother.~~ poor Daisy's mother. There is little to be added about the ~~with~~ incidental, but not unattractive Mr Hubert H. Hubert. He lodged for another happy year in that cosy house and died of a stroke in a hotel lift after a business dinner. Going up, one would like to surmise.

—.—

Two 18

she, Madame Lanskaya, did ressemble poor Daisy's mother.

There is little to add about the incidental, but not unat-tractive Mr Hubert H. Hubert. He lodged for another happy year in that cosy house and died of a stroke in a hotel lift after a business dinner. Going up, one would like to sur-mise.

Ch. Three

Flora was barely fourteen when she lost her virginity to a coeval, a handsome ballboy at the Carlton Courts in Cannes. Three or four broken porch steps — which was all that remained of an ornate public toilet, or some ancient templet — smothered in mints and campanulas and surrounded by junipers, formed the site of a duty she had resolved to perform rather than a casual pleasure she was now learning to taste. She observed with quiet interest the difficulty Jules had of drawing a junior-size sheath over an

---

Three 1

Ch. Three

Flora was barely fourteen when she lost her virginity to a coeval, a handsome ballboy at the Carlton Courts in Cannes. Three or four broken porch steps—which was all that remained of an ornate public toilet or some ancient templet—smothered in mints and campanulas and surrounded by junipers, formed the site of a duty she had resolved to perform rather than a casual pleasure she was now learning to taste. She observed with quiet interest the difficulty Jules had of drawing a junior-size sheath over an

----

ozgan that looked abnormally stout and had a at full erection head turned somewhat askew as if wary of receiving a backhand slap at the decisive moment. Flora let Jules do everything he desired except kiss her on the mouth, and the only words said referred to the next assignation.

¶ One evening after a hard day picking up and tossing balls and pattering in a crouch across court between the rallies of a long tournament the poor boy, stinking more than usual, pleaded

---

Three 2

organ that looked abnormally stout and at full erection had a head turned somewhat askew as if wary of receiving a backhand slap at the ~~decisive moment~~. Flora let Jules do everything he desired except kiss her on the mouth, and the only words said referred to the next assignation.

One evening after a hard day picking up and tossing balls and pattering in a crouch across court between the rallies of a long tournament the poor boy, stinking more than usual, pleaded

----

utter exhaustion and suggested going to a movie instead of making love; whereupon she walked away through the high heather and never saw Jules again — except when taking her tennis lessons with the stodgy old Basque in uncreased white trousers who had coached players in Odessa before World War One and still retained his effortless exquisite style.

¶ Back in Paris Flora found new lovers. With a gifted youngster from the Lanskaya school and another

---

Three 3

utter exhaustion and suggested going to a movie instead of making love; whereupon she walked away through the high heather and never saw Jules again—except when taking her tennis lessons with the stodgy old Basque in uncreased white trousers who had coached players in Odessa before World War One and still retained his effortless exquisite style.

Back in Paris Flora found new lovers. With a gifted youngster from the [Lanskaya] school and another

eager, more or less interchangeable couple
she would bycycle through the Blue Fountain
Forest to a romantic refuge where a
sparkle of broken glass or a lace-edged
rag on the moss were the only signs of
an earlier period of literature. A cloudless
September maddened the crickets. The girls
would compare the dimensions of their companions.
Exchanges would be enjoyed with giggles
and cries of surprise. Games of blindman's
buff would be played in the buff. Sometimes
a voyeur would be shaken out of a
tree by the vigilant police.

Three 4

---

eager, more or less interchangeable couple she would bycycle through the Blue Fountain Forest to a romantic refuge where a sparkle of broken glass or a lace-edged rag on the moss were the only signs of an earlier period of literature. A cloudless September maddened the crickets. The girls would compare the dimensions of their companions. Exchanges would be enjoyed with giggles and cries of surprise. Games of blindman's buff would be played in the buff. Sometimes a voyeur would be shaken out of a tree by the vigilant police.

¶   This is Flora of the close-set dark-blue ~~eyes~~ eyes and cruel mouth recollecting in her midtwenties fragments of her past, with details lost or put back in the wrong order, ~~TAIL between DELTA and SLIT~~, on dusty dim shelves, this is she. Everything about her is bound to remain blurry, even her name which seems to have been made expressly to have another one modelled upon it by a fantastically lucky artist. Of art, of love, of the

---

Three 5

This is Flora of the close-set dark-blue eyes and cruel mouth recollecting in her midtwenties fragments of her past, with details lost or put back in the wrong order, TAIL betwe[e]n DELTA and SLIT, on dusty dim shelves, this is she. Everything about her is bound to remain blurry, even her name which seems to have been made expressly to have another one modelled upon it by a fantastically lucky artist. Of art, of love, of the

----

difference between dreaming and waking she knew nothing but would have darted at you like a flatheaded blue serpent if you questioned her ~~meaning~~ ~~of dreaming,~~

Three 6

---

difference between dreaming and waking she knew nothing but would have darted at you like a flatheaded blue serpent if you questioned her.

She returned with her mother and Mr. Espenshade to Sutton, Mass. when she was born and now were to college in that town

At eleven she had read A quoi revent les enfants, by a certain Dr Freud, a madman.

St Leger d'Exu
The extracts came in a perse serie of Les great representat de notre epoque though why great represent wrote so badly remained was a mystery

Three 7

She returned with her mother and Mr. Espenshade to Sutton, Mass. where she was born and now went to college in that town.

At eleven she had read A quoi revent les enfants, by a certain Dr Freud, a madman.

The extracts came in a St Leger d'Exuperse series of Les great representant de notre epoque though why great represent[atives] wrote so badly remained a mystery

- - - - - - - - - - - - - - - - - -

Sutton College

Ex ◯

A sweet Japanese girl, who took Russian _and French_
because her stepfather was half French, and half Russian,
taught Flora to paint her left hand up to the radial
artery (one of the tenderest areas of her
beauty) with minuscule information, in
so called "fairy" script, regarding names, dates
and ideas. Both cheats had more French, than
Russian; _but_ in the latter the possible questions
formed, as it were, a banal bouquet of
probabilities: ~~————————————————~~

~~————————————————~~

Ex [o]

Sutton College

A sweet Japanese girl who took Russian and French
because her stepfather was half French and half Russian,
taught Flora to paint her left hand up to the radial artery
(one of the tenderest areas of her beauty) with minuscule
information, in so called "fairy" script, regarding names,
dates and ideas. Both cheats had more French, than Russian; but in the latter the possible questions formed, as it
were, a banal bouquet of probabilities:

Kind of

in Rus?)

What folklore preceded poetry; speak a little of
~~that~~ Lom. and Derzh.; paraphrase T's
letter to E.O.; what does I.I.'s doctor
deplore about the temperature of his own hands
when preparing to ___ his patient? — such
was the information demanded by the Profesor of Russian
Literature (a forlorn looking man bored
to extinction by his subject). As to the lady
who taught French Literature all she needed
were the names of modern French writers
and their listing on Flora's palm caused
a much denser tickle Especially memorable

Ex [1]

What kind of folklore preceded poetry in Rus?; speak a little of Lom. and Derzh.; paraphrase T's letter to E.O.; what
does I.I.'s doctor deplore about the temperature of his own
hands when preparing to [ ] his patient?—such was the
information demanded by the professor of Russian Literature (a forlorn looking man bored to extinction by his subject).* As to the lady who taught French Literature[,] all
she needed were the names of modern French writers and
their listing on Flora's palm caused a much denser tickle[.]
Especially memorable

*References are to Lomonosov and Derzhavin, Pushkin's Eugene Onegin and Tatanya, and Tol-
stoy's Ivan Ilyich; [ ] is used to indicate an intentional blank space throughout. —Dmitri Nabokov

----

little
was the cluster of interlocked names on the ball of
Flora's thumb: Malraux, Mauriac, Maurois, Michaux,
Michima, Montherland *and* Morand. What
amazes one is not the alliteration ~~on~~ (a joke
on the part of ~~the~~ a mannered alphabet);
not the inclusion of a foreign performer (a
joke on the part of that fun loving little
Japanese girld who would twist her
limbs into a pretzel when entertaining
Flora's Lesbian friends); and not even
the fact that virtually all those
writers were stunning mediocrities

Ex [2]

Modern French writers

---

was the little cluster of interlocked names on the ball of
Flora's thumb: Malraux, Mauriac, Maurois, Michaux,
Michima, Montherland and Morand. What amazes one is
not the alliteration (a joke on the part of a mannered alphabet); not the inclusion of a foreign performer (a joke on the
part of that fun loving little Japanese [girl] who would twist
her limbs into a pretzel when entertaining Flora's Lesbian
friends); and not even the fact that virtually all those writers were stunning mediocrities

----

as writers go (the first in the list being the worst) ; what amazes one is that they were supposed ~~should change to represent~~ to "represent an era" and that ~~the~~ such representants ~~genuine~~ could get away with the most execrable writing provided they represent their times.

Ex [3]

_____

as writers go (the first in the list being the worst); what
amazes one is that they were supposed to "represent an era"
and that such representants could get away with the most
execrable writing, provided they represent their times.

- - - - - - - - - - - - - - - - - - - -

Chapter Four

¶ Mrs Lanskaya died on the day her daughter graduated from Sutton College. A new fountain had just been bequeated to its campus by a former student, the widow of a shah. Generally speaking, one should carefully preserve in transliteration the feminine ending of a Russian surname (such as -aya, instead of the masculine -iy or -oy) when the woman in question is an artistic celebrity. So let it be "Landskaya" — land and sky and the melancholy echo

Four 1

Chapter Four

Mrs Lanskaya died on the day her daughter graduated from Sutton College. A new fountain had just been bequeat[h]ed to its campus by a former student, the widow of a shah. Generally speaking, one should carefully preserve in transliteration the feminine ending of a Russian surname (such as -<u>aya</u>, instead of the masculine -<u>iy</u> or -<u>oy</u>) when the woman in question is an artistic celebrity. So let it be "Landskaya"—land and sky and the melancholy echo

of her dancing name. The fountain took quite a time to get correctly erected after an initial series of unevenly spaced spasms. The potentate had been potent till the absurd age of eighty. It was a very hot day with its blue somewhat veiled. A few photographs moved among the crowd as indifferent to it as specters doing their spectral job. And certainly for no earthly reason does this passage ~~resembles of~~ ressemble in rythm ~~th~~ another novel,

Four 2

---

of her dancing name. The fountain took quite a time to get correctly erected after an initial series of unevenly spaced spasms. The potentate had been potent till the absurd age of eighty. It was a very hot day with its blue somewhat veiled. A few photograph[er]s moved among the crowd as indifferent to it as specters doing their spectral job. And certainly for no earthly reason does this passage ressemble in r[h]ythm another novel,

----

My Laura, where the mother appears as "Maya Umanskaya", a fabricated film actress.

Anyway, she suddenly collapsed on the lawn in the middle of the beautiful ceremony. A remarkable picture commemorated the event in "File". It showed Flora kneeling belatedly in the act of taking her mother's non-existent pulse, and it also showed a man of great corpulence and fame, still unacquainted with Flora: he stood just behind her, head bared and bowed, staring at the white of her

Four 3

My Laura, where the mother appears as "Maya Umanskaya", a fabricated film actress.

Anyway, she suddenly collapsed on the lawn in the middle of the beautiful ceremony. A remarkable picture commemorated the event in "File". It showed Flora kneeling belatedly in the act of taking her mother's non-existent pulse, and it also showed a man of great corpulence and fame, still unacquainted with Flora: he stood just behind her, head bared and bowed, staring at the white of her

- - - - - - - - - - - - - - - - - -

legs under her black gown and at the fair hair under her academic cap.

Four 4

---

legs under her black gown and at the fair hair under her academic cap.

Chaptn Five

¶ A brilliant neurologist, ~~a renowned~~ lecturer a gentleman of independent means, Dr Philip Wild had everything save an attractive exterior. However, one soon got over the shock of seeing that enormously fat creature mince toward the lectern on ridiculously small feet and of hearing the cock-a-doodle sound ~~with~~ which he cleared his throat before starting to enchant one with his ~~wit~~. Laura disregarded the wit but was mesmerized by his fame and fortune.

Five 1

Chapter Five

———————————

A brilliant neurologist, a renowned lecturer [and] a gentleman of independent means, Dr Philip Wild had everything save an attractive exterior. However, one soon got over the shock of seeing that enormously fat creature mince toward the lectern on ridiculously small feet and of hearing the cock-a-doodle sound with which he cleared his throat before starting to enchant one with his wit. Laura disregarded the wit but was mesmerized by his fame and fortune.

- - - - - - - - - - - - - - - - - -

¶ Fans were back that summer — the summer she made up her mind that the eminent Philip Wild, PH, would marry her. She had just opened a <u>boutique d'éventails</u> with another Sutton coed and the Polish artist Rawitch, pronounced by some Raw Itch, by him Rah Witch. Black fans and violet ones, fans like orange sunbursts, painted fans with clubtailed chinese butterflies oh they were a great hit, and one day Wild came and bought ~~five~~ (~~five~~ speading out her own fingers like pleats)

Five 2

Fans were back that summer—the summer she made up her mind that the eminent Philip Wild, PH, would marry her. She had just opened a <u>boutique d'éventails</u> with another Sutton coed and the Polish artist Rawitch, pronounced by some Raw Itch, by him Rah Witch. Black fans and violet ones, fans like orange sunbursts, painted fans with clubtailed Chinese butterflies oh they were a great hit, and one day Wild came and bought five (<u>five</u> spreading out her own fingers like pleats)

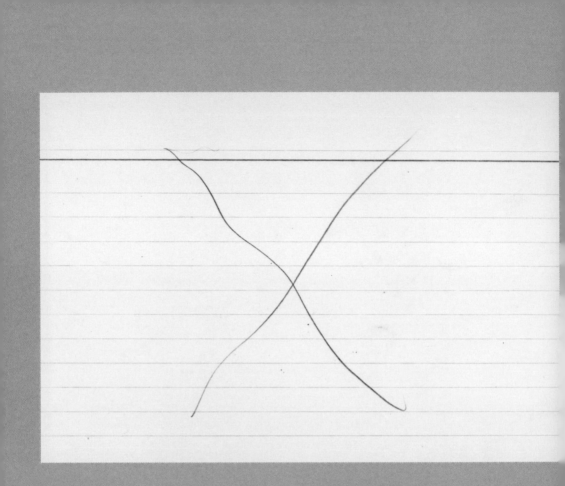

for " two aunts and three nieces " who did
not really exist, but never mind, it was
an unusual extravagance on his part
His shyness suprized and amused FLaura.
¶ Less amusing suprises awaited her.
To day after three years of marriage she
had enough of his fortune and fame.
He was a domestic miser. His New Jersey
house was absurdly understaffed. The
ranchito in Arizona had not been
redecorated for years. The villa on the

Five 3

---

for "two aunts and three nieces" who did not really exist,
but nevermind, it was an unusual extravagance on his
part[.] His shyness suprized and amused FLaura.

Less amusing surprises awaited her. To day after three
years of marriage she had enough of his fortune and
fame. He was a domestic miser. His New Jersey house was
absurdly understaffed. The ranchito in Arizona had not
been redecorated for years. The villa on the

Riviera had no swimming pool and only one bathroom. When she started to change all that, he would emit a kind of mild creak or squeak, and his brown eyes brimmed with sudden tears.

97

Five 4

Riviera had no swimming pool and only one bathroom. When she started to change all that, he would emit a kind of mild creak or squeak, and his brown eyes brimmed with sudden tears.

She saw their travels in terms of adverts and a long talcum-white beach with the tropical breeze tossing the palms and her hair; he saw it in terms of forbidden foods, frittered away time, and ghastly expenses.

Five 5

─────────────

She saw their travels in terms of adverts and a long talcum-white beach with the tropical breeze tossing the palms and her hair; he saw it in terms of forbidden foods, frittered away time, and ghastly expenses.

- - - - - - - - - - - - - - - - - -

Ivan Vaughan

chapter ~~five~~

The novel My ~~~~ Laura was begun very soon
after the end of the love affair it depicts,
was completed in one year ~~and~~ published
three months later. ~~and promptly torn apart~~
by a book reviewer in a leading newspaper.
It grimly survived and to the accompaniment
of muffled grunts on the part of the
librarious fates, its invisible hoisters, it
wriggled up to the top of the bestsellers' list
then started to slip, but stopped at a
~~midway~~ step in the vertical ice : A dozen

Five 1
Chapter [Five]*

Ivan Vaughan

The novel My <u>Laura</u> was begun very soon after the end of
the love affair it depicts, was completed in one year, published three months later[,] and promptly torn apart by a
book reviewer in a leading newspaper. It grimly survived
and to the accompaniment of muffled grunts on the part of
the librarious fates, its invisible hoisters, it wriggled up to
the top of the bestsellers' list then started to slip, but
stopped at a midway step in the vertical ice. A dozen

* This chapter was originally numbered as chapter five, but the author seems to have intended
to change its number.

Sundays passed and one had the impression that <u>Laura</u> had somehow got stuck on the seventh step (the last respectable one) or that, perhaps, some anonymous agent working for the author was buying up every week just enough copies to keep <u>Laura</u> there; but a day came when the climber above lost his foothold and toppled down disloging number seven and eight and nine in a general collapse beyond any hope of recovery.

Five 2

Sundays passed and one had the impression that <u>Laura</u> had somehow got stuck on the seventh step (the last respectable one) or that, perhaps, some anonymous agent working for the author was [buying] up every week just enough copies to keep <u>Laura</u> there; but a day came when the climber above lost his foothold and toppled down [dislodging] number seven and eight and nine in a general collapse beyond any hope of recovery.

- - - - - - - - - - - - - - - - - -

9. The "I" of the book is ~~crossed out~~ a neurotic and hesitant man of letters, who destroys his mistress in the act of portraying her. Statically — if one can put it that way — the portrait is a faithful one. Such fixed details as her trick of opening her mouth when toweling her inguen or of closing her eyes when smelling an inodorous rose are absolutely true to the original.

Five 3

The "I" of the book is a neurotic and hesitant man of letters, who destroys his mistress in the act of portraying her. Statically—if one can put it that way—the portrait is a faithful one. Such fixed details as her trick of opening her mouth when toweling her inguen or of closing her eyes when smelling an inodorous rose are absolutely true to the original.

- - - - - - - - - - - - - - - - -

spare prose of the author

Similarly

with its pruning of rich
adjectives

Similarly [the] spare prose of the author with its pruning of
rich adjectives

Philip Wild read "Laura" where
he is sympathically depicted as a conventional
"great "sientist" and though not a single
physical trait is mentiond, comes out
with astounding classical clarity.
under the name of ~~Phs~~ Philidor Sauvage
~~the~~

_____

Philip Wild read "Laura" where he is sympath[et]ically
depicted as a co[n]ventional "great s[c]ientist" and though
not a single physical trait is mentioned, comes out with
astounding classical clarity, under the name of Philidor
Sauvage

- - - - - - - - - - - - - - - - - - - -

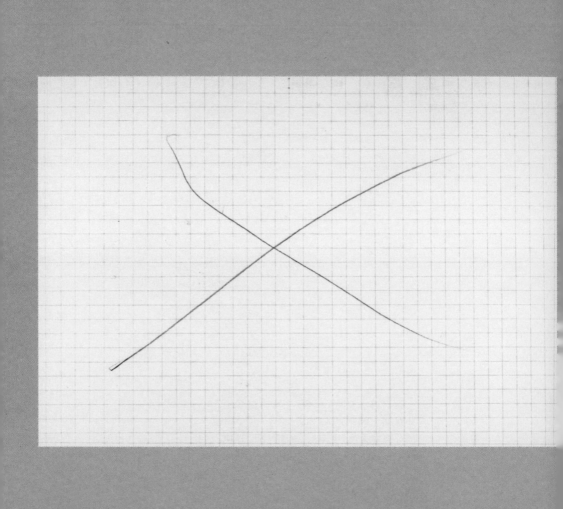

[handwritten note, circled top right: find substitute term for enkephalin]

[handwritten card:]

Times Dec. 18 75

"An enkephalin [c?] present in the brain has now been produced synthetically" "It is like morphine and other opiate drugs" Further research will show how and why "morphine has for centuries produced relief from pain and feelings of euphoria".

[invent tradename, e.g cephalopium]

[I taught thought to mimick an imperial neurotransmitter carrying my order of self destruction to my own brain. Suicide made a pleasure,

[Chapter Six]

Times Dec. 18 75

"An enk(c?)ephalin present in the brain has now been produced synthetically" "It is like morphine and other opiate drugs" Further research will show how and why "morphine has for centuries produced relief from pain and feelings of euphoria".

(invent tradename, e.g. cephalopium[;] find substitute term for enkephalin)

I taught thought to mimick an imperial neurotransmitter an aw[e]some messenger carrying my order of self destruction to my own brain. Suicide made a pleasure,

- - - - - - - - - - - - - - - - - -

its tempting emptiness

Do
_____

D
its tempting emptiness

The student who desires to die should learn first of all to project a mental image of himself upon his inner blackboard. This surface which at its virgin best has a dark-plum, rather than black, depth of opacity is none other than the underside of one's closed eyelids. To ensure a complete smoothness of background, care must be taken to eliminate the hypnagogic gargoyles and entoptic swarms which plague tired

D 1

Settling for a single line

The student who desires to die should learn first of all to project a mental image of himself upon his inner black-board. This surface which at its virgin best has a dark-plum, rather than black, depth of opacity is none other than the underside of one's closed eyelids.

To ensure a complete smoothness of background, care must be taken to eliminate the hypnagogic gargoyles and entoptic swarms which plague tired

----

vision after ~~meaning to~~ a surfeit (*ch.*) of poring over a collection of coins or insects. Sound sleep and an eyebath should be enough to cleanse the locus.

Now comes the mental image. In preparing for my own experiments — a long fumble which these notes shall ~~can~~ help novices to avoid — I toyed with the idea of drawing a fairly detailed, fairly recognizable portrait of myself on my private blackboard. I see myself

D 2

---

vision after a surfeit of poring over a collection of coins or insects. Sound sleep and an eyebath should be enough to cleanse the locus.

Now comes the mental image. In preparing for my own experiments—a long fumble which these notes shall help novices to avoid—I toyed with the idea of drawing a fairly detailed, fairly recognizable portrait of myself on my private blackboard. I see myself

----

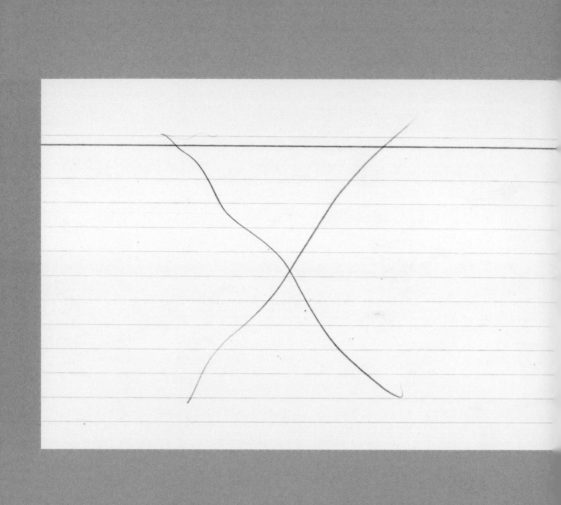

in my closet glass as an obese bulk
with formless features and
a sad porcine stare; but my visual
imagination is nil, and I am quite
unable to tuck Nigel Delling under my
eyelid, let alone keeping him there in
a fixed aspect of flesh for
any length of time. I then tried
various stylizations: a Delling-like doll,
a sketchy skeleton. Or would the
letters of my name do? Its recurrent "i"

D3

---

in my closet glass as an obese bulk with formless features
and a sad porcine stare; but my visual imagination is nil, I
am quite unable to tuck Nigel D[a]lling under my eyelid, let
alone keeping him there in a fixed aspect of flesh for any
length of time. I then tried various stylizations: a D[a]lling-
like doll, a sketchy skeleton. Or would the letters of my
name do? Its recurrent "i"

coinciding with our favorite pronoun) suggested an elegant solution: a simple vertical line across my field of inner vision could be chalked in an instant, and what is more I could mark lightly by transverse marks the three divisions of my physical self: legs, torso, and head ¶

D 4

---

coinciding with our favorite pronoun suggested an elegant solution: a simple vertical line across my field of inner vision could be chalked in an instant, and what is more I could mark lightly by transverse marks the three divisions of my physical self: legs, torso, and head

----

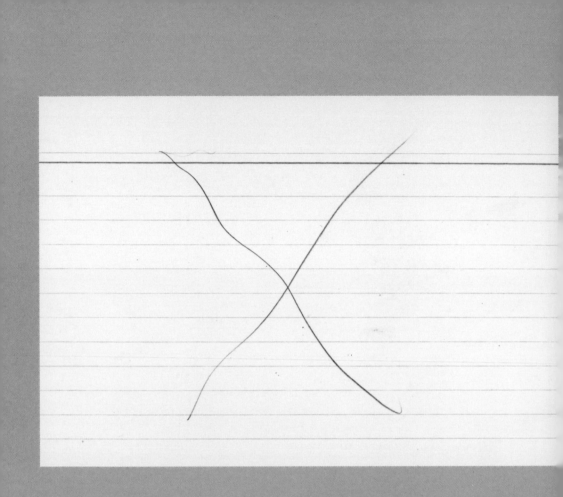

¶ Several months have now gone ~~passed~~ since I began working — not every day and not for protracted periods — on the upright line, emblemazing me. Soon, with the strong thumb of thought I could rub out its base, which corresponded to my joined feet. Being new to the process of self-deletion, I attributed the ecstatic relief of getting rid of my toes (as represented by the white pedicule I was erasing with more than masturbatory joy) to the fact that, ever since ~~illegible~~ I suffered torture

D 5

Several months have now gone since I began working—not every day and not for protracted periods—on the upright line emblemazing me. Soon, with the strong thumb of thought I could rub out its base, which corresponded to my joined feet. Being new to the process of self-deletion, I attributed the ecstatic relief of getting rid of my toes (as represented by the white pedicule I was erasing with more than masturbatory joy) to the fact that I suffered torture ever since

----

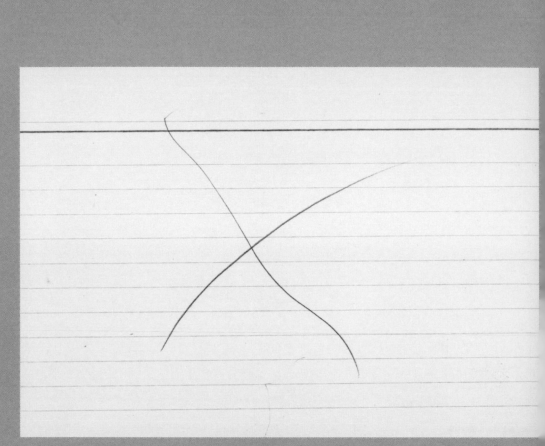

the sandals of childhood were replaced by
smart shoes, whose very polish reflected
pain and poison. So what a delight it
was to amputate my tiny feet! Yes, tiny,
yet I always wanted them, rolly polly dandy
that I am, to seem even smaller. The
daytime footware (chi) always hurt, always hurt.
~~when~~ I waddled home/ from work and
replaced the agony of my dapper oxfords by
the comfort of old bed slippers. This act of
mercy inevitably drew from me a voluptous

D 6

the sandals of childhood were replaced by smart shoes, whose very polish reflected pain and poison. So what a delight it was to amputate my tiny feet! Yes, tiny, yet I always wanted them, rolly polly dandy that I am, to seem even smaller. The daytime footware always hurt, always hurt. I waddled home from work and replaced the agony of my dapper oxfords by the comfort of old bed slippers. This act of mercy inevitably drew from me a volupt[u]ous

----

sigh which my wife, whenever I imprudently let her hear it, denounced as vulger, disgusting, obscene. Because see was a cruel lady or because she thought I might be clowning on purpose to irritate her, she once ~~or~~ hid my slippers, hid them furthermore in separate spot as one does with delicate siblings in ~~orphanages~~ orphanages, especially on chilly nights, but I forthwith went out and bought twenty pairs of soft, soft Carpetoes while hiding my tear-staining face under a Father Chrismas mask, which frightened the shopgirls.

D 7

sigh which my wife, whenever I imprudently let her hear it, denounced as vulgar, disgusting, obscene. Because [she] was a cruel lady or because she thought I might be clowning on purpose to irritate her, she once hid my slippers, hid them furthermore in separate spot[s] as one does with delicate siblings in orphanages, espccially on chilly nights, but I forthwith went out and bought twenty pairs of soft, soft Carpetoes while hiding my tear-staining face under a Father Chris[t]mas mask, which frightened the shopgirls.

For a moment I wondered with some apprehension if the deletion of my procreative system might produce nothing much more than a magnified orgasm. I was relieved to discover that the process continued sweet death's ineffable sensation which had nothing in common with ejaculations or sneezes. The three or four times that I reached that stage I forced myself to restore the lower half of my white "I" on my mental blackboard and thus wriggle out of my perilous trance.

D 8
The orange awnings of southern summers.

For a moment I wondered with some apprehension if the deletion of my procreative system might produce nothing much more than a magnified orgasm. I was relieved to discover that the process continued sweet death's ineffable sensation which had nothing in common with ejaculations or sneezes. The three or four times that I reached that stage I forced myself to restore the lower half of my white "I" on my mental blackboard and thus wriggle out of my perilous trance.

I, Philip Wild—

Lecturer in Experimental Psychology, University of Ganglia

I suffered for the last seventeen years from a humiliating stomach ailment which severely limited the jollities of companionship in small dining-rooms

---

D 9

I, Philip Wild[,] Lecturer in Experimental Psychology, University of Ganglia [, have] suffered for the last seventeen years from a humiliating stomack ailment which severely limited the jollities of companionship in small dining-rooms

- - - - - - - - - - - - - - - - - -

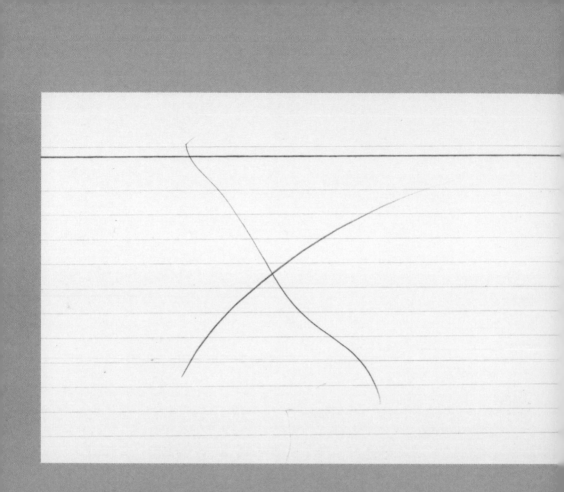

I loathe my belly, that trunkful of bowels, which) (I have to carry around, and everything connected with it — the wrong food, heartburn, consti-pation's leaden load, or else indigestion with a *first installment of* hot torrent of filth pouring out of me in a public toilet three minutes before a punctual engagement.

D 10

I loathe my belly, that trunkful of bowels, which I have to carry around, and everything connected with it—the wrong food, heartburn, constipation's leaden load, or else indigestion with a first installment of hot filth pouring out of me in a public toilet three minutes before a punctual engagement.

There is, there was, only one girl in my life, an object of terror and tenderness, an object too, of universal compassion on the part of millions who read about her in her lover's books. I say "girl" and not woman, not wife nor wench. If I were writing in my first language I would have said "fille". A sidewalk cafe, a summer-striped sunday: il regardait passer les filles. — that sense. Not professional whores, not necessarily well to-do tourists but "fille" as a translation of "girl" which I now retranslate:

D11

Heart (or Loins?)

There is, there was, only one girl in my life, an object of terror and tenderness, an object too, of universal compassion on the part of millions who read about her in her lover's books. I say "girl" and not woman, not wife nor wench. If I were writing in my first language I would have said "fille". A sidewalk cafe, a summer-striped sunday: il regardait passer les filles—that sense. Not professional whores, not necessarily well to-do tourists but "fille" as a translation of "girl" which I now retranslate:

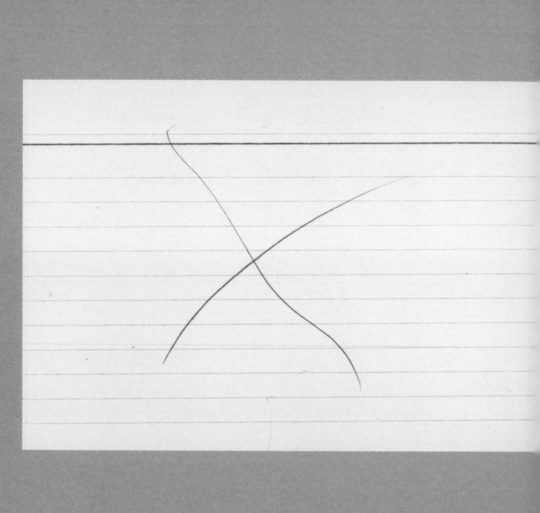

from heel to hip, then the trunk, then the head

A when so hig was
left but a grotesque
bust and with staring eyes

----

from heel to hip, then the trunk, then the head when nothing was left but a grotesque bust with staring eyes

----

Sophrosyne, a platonic term for ideal self-control stemming from man's rational core.

Sophrosyne, a platonic term for ideal self-control stemming from man's rational core.

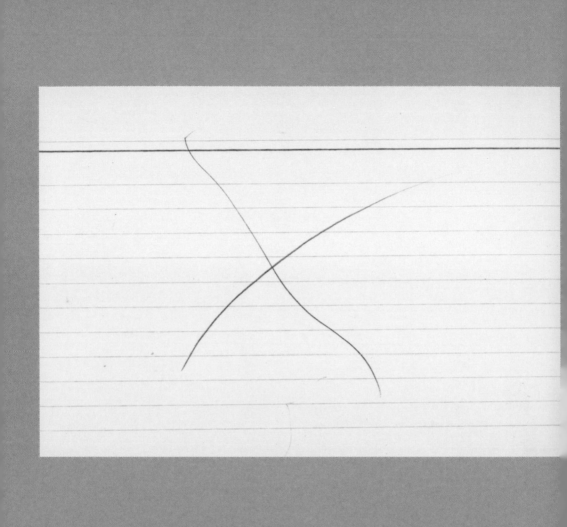

¶ I was enjoying a petit-beurre with my ~~noontime~~ *noontime* tea when the droll configuration of that particular bisquit's margins set into motion a train of thought that may have occurred to the reader even before it occurred to me. He knows already how much I disliked my toes. An ingrown nail on one foot and a a corn on the other were now pestering me. Would it no be a brilliant move, thought I to get rid of my toes by sacrificing them to an experiment that only

Wild [o]

[Chapter Seven]

I was enjoying a petit-beurre with my noontime tea when the droll configuration of that particular bisquit's margins set into motion a train of thought that may have occurred to the reader even before it occurred to me. He knows already how much I disliked my toes. An ingrown nail on one foot and a corn on the other were now pestering me. Would it no[t] be a brilliant move, thought I, to get rid of my toes by sacrificing them to an experiment that only

cowardness kept postponing? I had alwas
restored, on my mental blackboard, the
symbols of deleted organs before backing
out of my trance. Scientific curiousity
and plain logic demanded I prove
to myself that if I left the flawed
line alone, its flaw would be reflected in
the condition of this or that part of my
body. I dipped a last
petit-beurre in my tea, swallowed the
sweet mush and resolutely
started to work on my wretched flesh.

Wild [1]

cowardness kept postponing? I had alwa[y]s restored, on my mental blackboard, the symbols of deleted organs before backing out of my trance. Scientific curiousity and plain logic demanded I prove to myself that if I left the flawed line alone, its flaw would be reflected in the condition of this or that part of my body. I dipped a last petit-beurre in my tea, swallowed the sweet mush and resolutely started to work on my wretched flesh.

¶ Testing a discovery and finding it correct can be a great satisfaction but it can be also a great shock mixed with all the torments of rivalry and ignoble envy. I know ⟨at least two⟩ such rivals of mine —you, Curson, and you, Croydon— ⟨who⟩ will clap their claws like crabs ⟨in⟩ boiling water. Now when it is the discoverer himself who tests his discovery and finds that it works he will feel a torrent of pride and purity that will cause him

Wild [2]

Testing a discovery and finding it correct can be a great satisfaction but it can be also a great shock mixed with all the torments of rivalry and ignoble envy. I know at least two such rivals of mine—you, Curson, and you, Croydon—who will clap their claws like crabs in boiling water. Now when it is the discoverer himself who tests his discovery and finds that it works he will feel a torrent of pride and purity that will cause him

----

~~(crossed out text)~~ actually to
pity Prof. Curson and pet Dr. Croydon.
(whom I see Mr West has demolished in a
recent paper). We are above petty revenge.
¶ On a hot Sunday afternoon, in
my empty house — Flora and Cora being
somewhere in bed with their boyfriends —
I started the crucial test. The fine
base of my chalk white "I" was erased and
left erazed when I decided to break
my hypnotrance. The extermination of
my ten toes had been accompanied with

Wild [3]

actually to pity Prof. Curson and pet Dr. Croydon (whom I
see Mr West has demolished in a recent paper). We are
above petty revenge.

On a hot Sunday afternoon, in my empty house—Flora
and Cora being somewhere in bed with their boyfriends—I
started the crucial test. The fine base of my chalk white "I"
was erazed and left erazed when I decided to break my hypnotrance. The extermination of my ten toes had been
accompanied with

- - - - - - - - - - - - - - - - - -

the usual volupty. I was lying on a mattress in my bath, with the strong beam of my shaving lamp trained on my feet. When I opened my eyes, I saw at once that my toes were intact.

After swallowing my disappointment I scrambled out of the tub, landed on the tiled floor and fell on my face. To my intense joy I could not stand properly because my ten toes were in a state of indescribable numbness. They looked all right, though perhaps a

Wild [4]

----

the usual volupty. I was lying on a mattress in my bath, with the strong beam of my shaving lamp trained on my feet. When I opened my eyes, I saw at once that my toes were intact.

After swallowing my disappointment I scrambled out of the tub, landed on the tiled floor and fell on my face. To my intense joy I could not stand properly because my ten toes were in a state of indescribable numbness. They looked all right, though perhaps a

- - - - - - - - - - - - - - - - - -

a little paler than usual, but all sensation
had been slashed away by a razor of ice.
I palpated warily the hallux and the four
other digits of my right foot, then of my
left one and all was rubber and rot.
The immediate setting in of decay was especially
sensationally. I crept on all fours into
the adjacent bedroom and with infinite
effort into my bed.
        The rest was mere cleaning-up. In
the course of the night I teased off
the shrivelled white flesh and contemplated
with utmost delight

Wild [5]

---

a little paler than usual, but all sensation had been slashed
away by a razor of ice. I palpated warily the hallux and the
four other digits of my right foot, then of my left one and all
was rubber and rot. The immediate setting in of decay was
especially sensationally. I crept on all fours into the adjacent bedroom and with infinite effort into my bed.

The rest was mere cleaning-up. In the course of the
night I teased off the shrivelled white flesh and contemplated with utmost delight

[before his bath]

Will

I know my feet smelled despite daily baths, but this reek was something special

Wild [6]

I know my feet smelled despite daily baths, but <u>this</u> reek was something special

----

That test—though admittedly a trivial
affair—confirmed me in the belief that
I was working in the right direction
and that (unless some hideous wound
or excruciating sickness joined the
merry pallbearers) the process of dying
by auto-dissolution afforded the
greatest ecstasy known to man.

That test—though admittedly a trivial affair—confirmed
me in the belief that I was working in the right direction
and that (unless some hideous wound or excruciating sickness joined the merry pallbearers) the process of dying by
auto-dissolution afforded the greatest ecstasy known to
man.

Toes

I expected to see at best the length [of] each foot greatly reduced with its distal edge neatly transformed into the semblance of the end of a breadloaf without any trace of toes. At worst I was ready to face an anatomical prep[ar]ation of ten bare phalanges sticking out of my feet like a skeleton's claws. Actually all I saw was the familiar rows of digits.

- - - - - - - - - - - - - - - - - -

¶ " Install yourself ", said the youngish suntanned, cheerful ðε Aupert, indicating, openheartedly an armchair at the north rim of his desk, and proceeded to explain the necessity of a surgical intervention. He showed A.N.D. one of the dark grim urograms that had been taken of A.N.D.'s rear anatomy. The globular shadow of an adenoma eclipsed the greater part of the whitish bladder. This

1

Medical Intermezzo

"Install yourself," said the youngish suntanned, cheerful Dr Aupert, indicating openheartedly an armchair at the north rim of his desk, and proceeded to explain the necessity of a surgical intervention. He showed A.N.D. one of the dark grim urograms that had been taken of A.N.D.'s rear anatomy. The globular shadow of an adenoma eclipsed the greater part of the whitish bladder. This

a ~~~~ benign tumor ~~has~~ had been growing
on the prostate for some fifteen years
and was now as many times its size
The unfortunate gland ~~~~
with the great gray parisite clinging
to it could and should be removed at once
"And if I refuse? said AND
"Then, one of these days,

2

---

benign tumor had been growing on the prostate for some
fifteen years and was now as many times its size. The unfortunate gland with the great gray par[a]site clinging to it
could and should be removed at once
    "And if I refuse? said AND.
    "Then, one of these days,

- 177 -

that back[grd] keep it free from any intervention. tired eyes.

　　　Such as hypnagogic gargoyles* or entoptic swarms*
　　　a vertical line chalked against a plum* tinted darkness
　　　over one's collection of coins or insects
　　　a manikin or a little skeleton but that demanded

* These phrases appear as well on page 131, which may indicate that this card is a draft of that material.

very special

In this [self-hypnotic state] there can be no question of getting out of touch with onself and floating into a normal sleep (unless you are very tired at the start)

To break the trance all you do is to restore in ~~all its~~ ^every^ chalk-bright details the simple picture of yourself ^a stylized skeleton^ on your mental blackboard. One should remember, however, that the divine delight in destroying, say one's breastbone should not be indulged in. Enjoy the destruction but do not linger over your own ruins lest you develop ~~an incurable~~ illness, or die before you are ready to die.

In this very special self-hypnotic state there can be no question of getting out of touch with on[e]self and floating into a normal sleep (unless you are very tired at the start)

To break the trance all you do is to restore in every chalk-bright details the simple picture of yourself a stylized skeleton on your men[t]al blackboard. One should remember, however, that the divine delight in destroying, say[,] one's breastbone should not be indulged in. Enjoy the destruction but do not linger over your own ruins lest you develop an incurable illness, or die before you are ready to die.

- - - - - - - - - - - - - - - - - -

the delight of getting under ~~beneath~~
of an ingrown toe nail with a sharp scissor
and snipping off the offending corner
and the added ecstasy of finding beneath it
an amber abcess whose blood flows
carrying away of the ignoble pain

But with age I could not
bend any longer toward my feet
and was ashamed to present
them to a pedicure.

---

the delight of getting under an ingrown toenail with sharp scissors and snipping off the offending corner and the added ecstasy of finding beneath it an amber ab[s]cess whose blood flows[,] carrying away the ignoble pain

But with age I could not bend any longer toward my feet and was ashamed to present them to a pedicure.

Last Chapter
Beginning of last chapter

[Miss Ure, this is the MS of my last chapter which you will, please, type out in three copies—I need the additional one for prepub in <u>Bud</u>—or some other magasine.]*

Several years ago, when I was still working at the Horloge Institute of Neurologie, a silly female interviewer introduced me in a silly radio series ("Modern Eccentrics") as "a gentle Oriental sage, founder of

*Brackets around the first paragraph may be a reminder to set it as extract.

End of penult chapter.

The manuscript in longhand of Wild's last chapter, which at the time of his fatal heart attack, ten blocks away, his typist, Sue U, had not had the time to tackle because of urgent work for another employer was deftly plucked from her hand by that other fellow to find a place of publication more permanent than Bud or Root.

—

Penult. End.

End of penult chapter.

The manuscript in longhand of Wild's last chapter, which at the time of his fatal heart attack, ten blocks away, his typist, Sue U, had not had the time to tackle because of urgent work for another employer[,] was deftly plucked from her hand by that other fellow to find a place of publication more permanent than <u>Bud</u> or <u>Root</u>.

—

- - - - - - - - - - - - - - - - - -

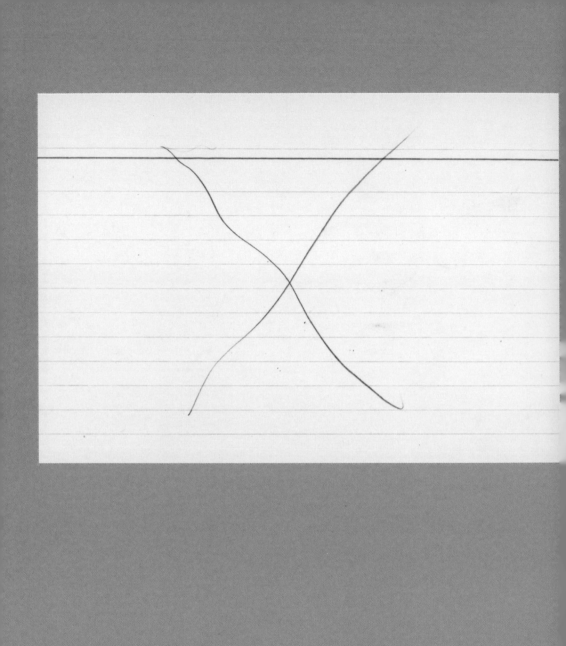

already
Well, a writer of sorts. A budding and
a right rotting writer. After being a poor
lector in some of our last dreary castles.
Yes, he's a lecturer too A rich rotten
lecturer (complete misunderstanding, another world)
Whom are they talking about? Her
husband I guess. Flo is horribly frank
about Philipp. (who could not come to
the party. — to any party)

First a

Well, a writer of sorts. A budding and already rotting
writer. After being a poor lector in some of our last dreary
castles.

Yes, he's a lecturer too[.] A rich rotten lecturer (complete misunderstanding, another world).

Whom are they talking about? Her husband I guess. Flo
is horribly frank about Philipp. (who could not come to the
party—to any party)*

* This material fits in with conversation in the first chapter.

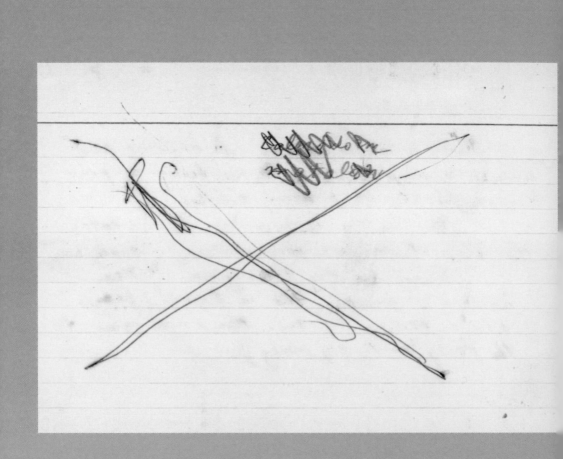

First b

_____

heart or brain—when the ray projected by me reaches the lake of Dante [or] the Island of Reil

- - - - - - - - - - - - - - - - - -

Wild: I do not believe that ~~they~~ the spinal cord is the only or even main conductor of the extravagant messages that reach my brain. I have to find out more about that — about the strange impression I have of there being some underpath, so to speak, along which the commands of my will power are passed to and fro along the shadow of nerves, rather along the nerves proper.

First c

Thornton + Smart <u>Hum</u>. <u>Physiology</u>

p. 299

Wild's [ms.]: I do not believe that the spinal cord is the only or even main conductor of the extravagant messages that reach my brain. I have to find out more about that— about the strange impression I have of there being some underpath, so to speak, along which the commands of my will power are passed to and fro along the shadow of nerves, rather [than] along the nerves proper.

The photograph~~er~~ was setting up

I alway know she is cheating on me with a new boy-friend whenever she visits my bleak bedroom more often then once a month (which is the average since I turned sixty)

First d

The photograph[er] was setting up

    I alway[s] know she is cheating on me with a new boy friend whenever she visits my bleak bedroom more often than once a month (which is the average since I turned sixty)

The only way he could possess her was
in the most   position of copulation:
he reclining on cushions, she   sitting in
the fauteuil of his flesh with her back to
him.   ¶   The procedure — a few bounces
over very small humps — meant nothing to her.
She looked at : f the snow-scape on the
footboard of the bed — h;
at the   curtains
; and he holding her in front of him like a
child being given a sleigh ride down a

I

The only way he could possess her was in the most [   ]
position of copulation: he reclining on cushions: she sitting in the fauteuil of his flesh with her back to him. The
procedure—a few bounces over very small humps—meant
nothing to her[.] She looked at the snow-scape on the footboard of the bed—at the [curtains]; and he holding her in
front of him like a child being given a sleighride down a

- - - - - - - - - - - - - - - - - -

short slope by a kind stranger,
he saw her [lyric] back, her
hip between his hands.

Like toads or tortoises neither saw each
other's faces   See animaux

II

---

short slope by a kind stranger, he saw her back, her hip[s]
between his hands.

Like toads or tortoises neither saw each other's faces
See <u>animaux</u>

(Wild's notes)

My sexual life is virtually over but —

I saw you again, Aurora Lee, whom
as a youth I had pursued with hopeless desire
at high-school balls — and whom I have cornered now
fifty years later, on a terrace of my
dream .: Your painted pout and cold
gaze were, come to think of it, very like
the official lips and eyes of Flora, my
wayward wife, and your flimsy
frock of black silk might have come
from her recent wardrobe. You turned
away, but could not escape, trapped

Aurora 1
Wild's notes

My sexual life is virtually over but—

I saw you again, Aurora Lee, whom as a youth I had pursued with hopeless desire at high-school balls—and whom I have cornered now fifty years later, on a terrace of my dream. Your painted pout and cold gaze were, come to think of it, very like the official lips and eyes of Flora, my wayward wife, and your flimsy frock of black silk might have come from her recent wardrobe. You turned away, but could not escape, trapped

as you were among the
close-set columns of moonlight and I
lifted the hem of your dress — something I never had done in the past — and stroked,
moulded, pinched ever so softly your pale
prominent nates, while you stood perfectly still
as if considering new possibilities of
power and pleasure and interior decoration.
At the height of your guarded ecstasy I thrust
my cupped hand from behind between your consenting
thighs and felt the
sweat-stuck folds of a long scrotum and

Aurora 2

as you were among the close-set columns of moonlight and I lifted the hem of your dress—something I never had done in the past—and stroked, moulded, pinched ever so softly your pale prominent nates, while you stood perfectly still as if considering new possibilities of power and pleasure and interior decoration. At the height of your guarded ecstasy I thrust my cupped hand from behind between your consenting thighs and felt the sweat-stuck folds of a long scrotum and

then, further in front, the droop of a
short member. Speaking as an authority on
dreams, I wish to add that this was
no homosexual manifestation but a
splendid example of terminal gynandrism.
Young Aurora Lee (who was to be
axed and chopped up at seventeen by an
idiot lover, all glasses and beard)
and half-impotent old Wild formed
for a moment one creature. But quite
apart from all that, in a more

Aurora 3

then, further in front, the droop of a short member. Speaking as an authority on dreams, I wish to add that this was no
homosexual manifestation but a splendid example of terminal gynandrism. Young Aurora Lee (who was to be axed
and chopped up at seventeen by an idiot lover, all glasses
and beard) and half-impotent old Wild formed for a
moment one creature. But quite apart from all that, in a
more

disgusting and delicious sense, her little bottom, so smooth, so moonlit, a replica, in fact, of her twin brother's charms, ~~samfled~~ sampled rather brutally on my last night at boarding school, ~~~~ remained inset in the medalion of every following day.

Aurora 4

disgusting and delicious sense, her little bottom, so smooth, so moonlit, a replica, in fact, of her twin brother's charms, sampled rather brutally on my last night at boarding school, remained inset in the medal[l]ion of every following day.

Willpower, absolute self domination.

Electroencephalographic recordings of the hypnotic "sleep" are very similar to those of the waking state and quite different from those of normal sleep; yet there are certain minute details about the pattern of the trance which are of extraordinary interest and place it specifically apart from sleeping and worrying.

Miscel.

Willpower, absolute self domination.

Electroencephalographic recordings of hypnotic "sleep" are very similar to those of the waking state and quite different from those of normal sleep; yet there are certain minute details about the pattern of the trance which are of extraordinary interest and place it specifically apart both from sleep and [waking].

self-extinction
self-immolation, -tor

Wild's note

Three card at least of this stuff

As I destroyed my thorax, I also destroyed
and the
and the laughing people in theaters with a
not longer visible stage or screen, and
the
and the   in the cemetery
of the asymetrical heart

autosuggestion, autosugetist
autosuggestive

Wild's note

---

self-extinction
self-immolation, -tor
    As I destroyed my thorax, I also destroyed [ ] and the
[ ] and the laughing people in theaters with a not longer
visible stage or screen, and the [ ] and the [ ] in the cemetery of the asym[m]etrical heart
autosuggestion, autosugetist
autosuggestive

A process of self-obliteration conducted by an effort of ~~the~~ will. ~~The~~ pleasure, bordering on almost ~~unendurable~~ exstacy, comes from feeling the will working at a ~~completely~~ new task: an act of destruction which develops paradoxically an element of creativeness in the totally new application of totally free will. Learning to use the vigor of the body ~~for the purpose of its own deletion~~ standing vitality on its head.

Wild's notes

A process of self-obliteration conducted by an effort of the will. Pleasure, bordering on almost unendurable ex-stacy, comes from feeling the will working at a new task: an act of destruction which develops paradoxically an element of creativeness in the totally new application of totally free will. Learning to use the vigor of the body for the purpose of its own deletion[,] standing vitality on its head.

- - - - - - - - - - - - - - - - - -

Nirvana blowing out, [extinguishing],
extinction, disappearance in Buddhist
theology extinction ... and absorption into
the supreme spirit.
[nirvanic embrace of Brahma]
bonze = Buddhist monk
bonzery, bonzeries
the doctrine of Buddhist incarnation,
Brahmahood = absorption into the divine
essence.
Brahmism
[all this postulates a supreme god]

OED

_____

Nirvana [ ] blowing out (extinguishing), extinction, disappearance. In Buddhist theology extinction . . . and absorption into the supreme spirit.

(nirvanic embrace of Brahma)
bonze = Buddhist monk
bonzery, bonzeries
the doctrine of Buddhist incarnation
Brahmahood = absorption into the divine essence.
Brahmism
(all this postulates a supreme god)

Buddhism

    Nirvana = "extinction of the self" "individual existence"
    "release from the cycle of incarnations"
    "reunion with Brahma (<u>Hinduism</u>)
    attained through the suppression of individ[ual] existence.

<u>Buddhism</u>: Beatic spiritual condition

    The religious rubbish and mysticism of Oriental wisdom

    The minor poetry of mystical myths

The novel <u>Laura</u> was sent to me by the painter Rawitch, a ~~rejected~~ admirer of my wife, of whom he did an exquisite oil a few years ago. The way I was led by delicate clues and ghostly nudges to the exhibition where "Lady with Fan" was sold to me by his girl friend, a sniggering tart with gilt fingernails, is a separate anecdote in the anthology of humiliation to which, since my marriage, I have been a constant contributor. As to the book,

Wild A

The novel <u>Laura</u> was sent to me by the painter Rawitch, a rejected admirer of my wife, of whom he did an exquisite oil a few years ago. The way I was led by delicate clues and ghostly nudges to the exhibition where "Lady with Fan" was sold to me by his girlfriend, a sniggering tart with gilt fingernails, is a separate anecdote in the anthology of humiliation to which, since my marriage, I have been a constant contributor. As to the book,

- - - - - - - - - - - - - - - - - -

a bestseller, ^{which} ̶x̶ the̶ a̶ blurb described ̶&̶ as
" a roman à clef with the <u>clef</u> lost for
ever", the demonic hands of one of
my servants, ̶t̶h̶e̶ Velvet Valet - ̶a̶s̶ ̶m̶e̶
Flora called him, kept ̶s̶l̶i̶p̶p̶i̶n̶g̶ it
into my visual field until I
opened the damned thing and discovered
it to be a maddening masterpiece

Wild B

---

a bestseller, which the blurb described as "a roman à clef
with the <u>clef</u> lost for ever", the demonic hands of one of my
servants, the Velvet Valet as Flora called him, kept slipping
it into my visual field until I opened the damned thing and
discovered it to be a maddening masterpiece

- - - - - - - - - - - - - - - - - -

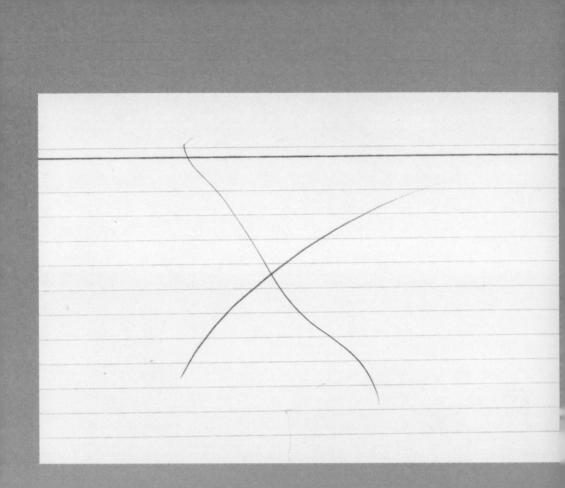

¶¶ Winny Carr waiting for her train on the station platform of Sex, a delightful Swiss resort famed for its crimson plums noticed her old friend Flora on a bench near the bookstall with a paperback in her lap. This was the soft cover copy of Laura issued virtually at the same time as its much stouter and comelier hardback edition. She had just bought it at the station bookstall,

Z

Last §

Winny Carr waiting for her train on the station platform of Sex, a delightful Swiss resort famed for its crimson plums[,] noticed her old friend Flora on a bench near the bookstall with a paperback in her lap. This was the soft cover copy of <u>Laura</u> issued virtually at the same time as its much stouter and comelier hardback edition. She had just bought it at the station bookstall,

- - - - - - - - - - - - - - - - - -

and in answer to Winny's jocular remark
(" hope you'll enjoy the story of your
life ") said she doubted if she could
force herself to start reading it.
        Oh you must! said Winnie,
it is of course, fictionalized and all
that but ~~as Tony says~~ ~~pretty~~
you'll come ~~to~~ face to face with yourself ~~at~~
~~...~~
~~...~~ ~~your~~
~~...~~ at every other corner And
there's your wonderful death. Let me

Z2

---

and in answer to Winny's jocular remark ("hope you'll
enjoy the story of your life") said she doubted if she could
force herself to start reading it.

    Oh you must! said Winnie, it is, of course, fictionalized
and all that but you'll come face to face with yourself at
every other corner. And there's your wonderful death. Let
me

----

show you your wonderful death. Damn, here's my train. Are we going together?
"I'm not going anywhere. I'm expecting somebody. Nothing very exciting. Please, let me have my book.'
" Oh, but I simply must find that passage for you. It's not quite at the end. You'll scream with laughter. Its the craziest death in the world.
"You'll miss your train" said Flora

Z_3

---

show you your wonderful death. Damn, here's my train. Are
we going together?["]

"I'm not going anywhere. I'm expecting somebody.
Nothing very exciting. Please, let me have my book."

"Oh, but I simply must find that passage for you. It's not
quite at the end. You'll scream with laughter. It's the craziest
death in the world.["]

"You'll miss your train" said Flora

- - - - - - - - - - - - - - - - - -

Philip Wild spent most of the afternoon in the shade of a marbrosa tree (that he vaguely mistook for an opulent ~~trunk~~ ~~an~~ tropical race of the birch) sipping tea with lemon and ~~spreading~~ making ~~know~~ embryonic notes ~~attached to a pen~~ ~~which~~, with a diminutive pencil attached to ~~a~~ diminutive agenda-book which seemed to melt into his broad moist palm ~~where it would~~ spread ~~in~~ sporadic crucifixions. He sat ~~with~~ widespread

Five A

Philip Wild spent most of the afternoon in the shade of a <u>marbrosa</u> tree (that he vaguely mistook for an opulent tropical race of the birch) sipping tea with lemon and making embryonic notes with a diminutive pencil attached to a diminutive agenda-book which seemed to melt into his broad moist palm where it would spread in sporadic crucifixions. He sat with widespread

- - - - - - - - - - - - - - - - - -

legs to accomodate his enormous stomack and now and then checked or made in midthought half a movement to check the fly buttons of his old fashioned white trousers. There was also the recurrent search for his pencil sharpener, which he absently pat into a different pocket every time after use. Otherwise, between all those small movements, he sat perfectly still, like a meditative idol. Flora would be often present lolling in a deckchair,

Five B

---

legs to accom[m]odate his enormous stomack and now and then checked or made in midthought half a movement to check the fly buttons of his old fashioned white trousers. There was also the recurrent search for his pencil sharpener, which he absently put into a different pocket every time after use. Otherwise, between all those small movements, he sat perfectly still, like a meditative idol. Flora would be often present lolling in a deckchair,

----

enclosing his chair in a *her progression* of strewn magazines C

moving it from time to time, circling as it were around her husband, *and* ~~in quest of~~ *as she sought* an even denser shade than the one sheltering him. The urge to expose the maximum of naked flesh permitted by fashion was combined in her strange little mind with a *dread of the* least touch of tan ~~as~~ defiling her ivory skin

C

---

moving it from time to time, circling as it were around her husband, and enclosing his chair in her progression of strewn magazines as she sought an even denser shade than the one sheltering him. The urge to expose the maximum of naked flesh permitted by fashion was combined in her strange little mind with a dread of the least touch of tan defiling her ivory skin.

To all contraceptive precautions, and indeed to orgasm at its safest and deepest, I much preferred — madly preferred —, finishing off at my ease against the softest part of her thigh. This predilection might have ~~been~~ due to the unforgettable impact of my ~~romps~~ with schoolmates of different but erotically identical, sexes

Eric's notes

To all contraceptive precautions, and indeed to orgasm at its safest and deepest, I much preferred—madly preferred—finishing off at my ease against the softest part of her thigh. This predilection might have been due to the unforgettable impact of my romps with schoolmates of different but erotically identical, sexes

----

he too needed
and that he would come to stay for for at least a week every
other month

This [key] for a Theme
Begin with [poem] etc and
finish with mast and Flora, ascribe to picture

After a three-year separation (distant war,
regular exchange of tender letters) we met
again. Though still married to that hog she
kept away from him and at the moment
sojourned at a central European resort
in eccentric solitude. We met in a
splendid park that she praised with
exaggerated warmth — picturesque trees,
blooming meadows — and in a secluded
part of it an ancient "~~parolin~~ rotonda"
with pictures and music" where ~~and~~

X

After a three-year separation (distant war, regular
exchange of tender letters) we met again. Though still
married to that hog she kept away from him and at the
moment sojourned at a central European resort in eccentric solitude. We met in a splendid park that she praised
with ⌊exaggerated⌋ warmth—picturesque trees, blooming
meadows—and in a secluded part of it an ancient "rotonda"
with pictures and music where

we simply had to stop for a rest and a
bite — the sisters, I mean, she said, the attendant
there — served iced coffee and cherry
tart of quite special quality — and
as she spoke I suddenly began to
realise with a sense of utter depression
and embarrassment that the "pavillion"
was ~~the was~~ the celebrated Green Chapel
of St Esmeralda
and that she was brimming with religious
~~fervor~~ and yet miserably, desperately fearful, despite
bright smiles and ~~an air enjoué~~, of my
insulting her by some mocking remark.

---

we simply had to stop for a rest and a bite—the sisters, I
mean, she said, the attendant[s] there—served iced coffee
and cherry tart of quite special quality—and as she spoke I
suddenly began to realise with a sense of utter depression
and embarrassment that the "pavillion" was the celebrated
Green Chapel of St Esmeralda and that she was brimming
with religious fervor and yet miserably, desperately fearful,
despite bright smiles and <u>un air enjoué</u>, of my insulting her
by some mocking remark.

\- - - - - - - - - - - - - - - - -

The wall did not go up to the ceiling. It stopped at the magenta horizon of its own painted verge, where the terraced slope of the white-washed ceiling used to begin go

¶ I hit upon the art of thinking away my body, my being, mind itself. To think away thought — luxurious suicide, delicious dissolution! Dissolution, in fact, is a marvelously apt term here, for as you sit relaxed in this comfortable chair (narrator striking its armrests) and start destroying yourself, the first thing you feel is a mounting melting, from the feet upward

D o

I hit upon the art of thinking away my body, my being, mind itself. To think away thought—luxurious suicide, delicious dissolution! Dissolution, in fact, is a marvelously apt term here, for as you sit relaxed in this comfortable chair (narrator striking its armrests) and start destroying yourself, the first thing you feel is a mounting melting from the feet upward

- - - - - - - - - - - - - - - - - - -

In experimenting on oneself in order to
pick out the sweetest death, one cannot,
obviously, set a part of one's body on fire
or drain it of blood or subject it to any other
drastic operation, for the simple reason that
these are one-way treatments: ~~all~~ there is
no resurrecting the organ one has
destroyed. It is the ability to stop the
experiment and return intact from the
perilous journey that makes all the difference,
once ~~learning~~ its mysterious technique

D one

In experimenting on oneself in order to pick out the
sweetest death, one cannot, obviously, set part of one's
body on fire or drain it of blood or subject it to any other
drastic operation, for the simple reason that these are one-
way treatments: there is no resurrecting the organ one has
destroyed. It is the ability to stop the experiment and return
intact from the perilous journey that makes all the difference, once its mysterious technique

----

has been mastered by the student of self-annihilation. From the preceding chapters and the footnotes to them, he has learned, I hope, how to put himself into neutral, i.e. into a harmless trance and how to get out of it by a resolute wrench of the watchful will. What cannot be taught is the specific method of dissolving one's body, or at least part of one's body, while tranced. A deep probe of one's darkest self, the unraveling of subjective associations, may suddenly

D two

---

has been mastered by the student of self-annihilation. From the preceding chapters and the footnotes to them, he has learned, I hope, how to put himself into neutral, i.e. into a harmless trance and how to get out of it by a resolute wrench of the watchful will. What cannot be taught is the specific method of dissolving one's body, or at least part of one's body, while tranced. A deep probe of one's darkest self, the unraveling of subjective associations, may suddenly

----

lead to the shadow of a clue and then to the clue itself. The only help I can provide is not even paradigmatic. For all I know, the way I found to woo death may be quite atypical; yet the story has to be told for the sake of its strange logic.

In a recurrent dream of my childhood I used to see a ssmudge on the wallpaper or on a whitewashed door, a nasty smudge that started to come alive,

D three

lead to the shadow of a clue and then to the clue itself. The only help I can provide is not even paradigmatic. For all I know, the way I found to woo death may be quite atypical; yet the story has to be told for the sake of its strange logic.

In a recurrent dream of my childhood I used to see a smudge on the wallpaper or on a whitewashed door, a nasty smudge that started to come alive,

----

turning into a crustacean-like monster. As its appendages began to move, a thrill of foolish horror shook me awake; but the same night or the next I would be again facing idly some wall or screen on which a spot of dirt would attract the naive sleeper's attention by starting to grow and make groping and clasping gestures — and again I managed to wake up before its bloated bulk got unstuck from the wall. But one night

---

D four

---

turning into a crustacean-like monster. As its appendages began to move, a thrill of foolish horror shook me awake; but the same night or the next I would be again facing idly some wall or screen on which a spot of dirt would attract the naive sleeper's attention by starting to grow and make groping and clasping gestures—and again I managed to wake up before its bloated bulk got unstuck from the wall. But one night

---

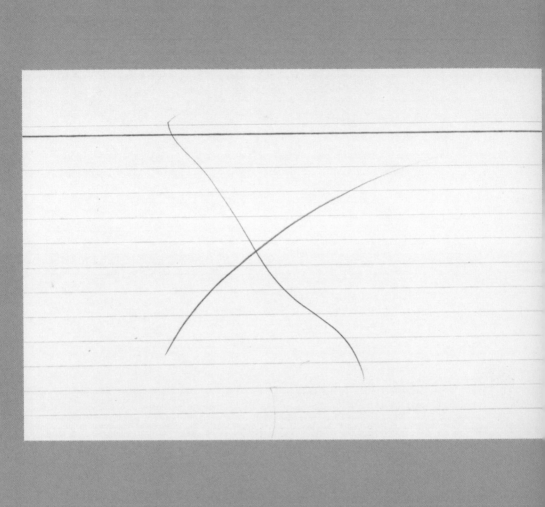

when some trick of position, some dimple
of pillow, some fold of bedclothes made
me feel brighter and braver than usual,
I let the smudge start its evolution
and, drawing on an imagined mitten, I simply
rubbed out the beast. Three or four times
it appeared again in my dreams but
now I welcomed its growing shape and
gleefully erased it. Finally it gave up
~~coming as~~ — as some day life will give up —
bothering me.

D five

when some trick of position, some dimple of pillow, some
fold of bedclothes made me feel brighter and braver than
usual, I let the smudge start its evolution and, drawing on
an imagined mitten, I simply rubbed out the beast. Three
or four times it appeared again in my dreams but now I welcomed its growing shape and gleefully erased it. Finally it
gave up—as some day life will give up—bothering me.

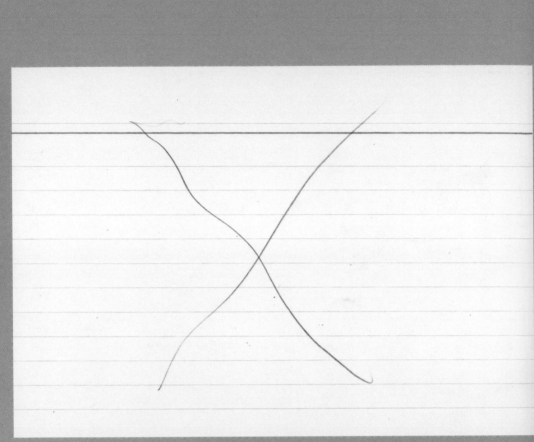

¶ I have never derived the least joy from my legs. In fact I strongly object to the bipedal condition The fatter and wiser I grew the more I abominated the task of grappling with ~~long~~ Drawers, trousers and pyjama pants. Had I been able to bear the stink and stickiness of my own ~~unwashed~~ body I would have slept ~~apparently~~ ~~staying~~ with all my clothes on and had ~~a~~ valets—~~preferably~~ with some experience in the tailoring of corpses — ~~~~ change me, say, once a week. But then,

Legs 1   7

I have never derived the least joy from my legs. In fact I strongly object to the bipedal condition[.] The fatter and wiser I grew the more I abominated the task of grappling with long drawers, trousers and pyjama pants. Had I been able to bear the stink and stickiness of my own unwashed body I would have slept with all my clothes on and had valets—preferably with some experience in the tailoring of corpses—change me, say, once a week. But then,

----

- 255 -

I also loath ~~necessaryness~~, the proximity
of valets and the vile touch of their
hands. The last one I had was at
least clean ~~~~~~~~~ but he regarded
the act of dressing his master as a battle
of wits, he doing his best ~~~~~~
~~~~~~~~~~~~~~~~~~~~~~~~~
to turn the wrong outside ~~into~~ the
right inside and I undoing his endeavors
by working my right foot into my
left trouser leg. Our complicated
exertions, which to an onlooker might

Legs 2   8

I also loath[e] the proximity of valets and the vile touch of
their hands. The last one I had was at least clean but he
regarded the act of dressing his master as a battle of wits, he
doing his best to turn the wrong outside into the right
inside and I undoing his endeavors by working my right
foot into my left trouser leg. Our complicated exertions,
which to an onlooker might

- - - - - - - - - - - - - - - - -

have seemed some sort of exotic wrestling
match. Would take us from one
room to another and end by my
sitting on the floor, exhausted and
hot, with the bottom of my trousers
mis-clothing my heaving abdomen.
      Finally, in my sixties, I
found the right person to dress and
undress me; an old illusionist
who is able to go behind a
screen in the guise of a cossack and
instantly come out at the other end as

Legs 3   9

have seemed some sort of exotic wrestling match[,] would
take us from one room to another and end by my sitting
on the floor, exhausted and hot, with the bottom of my
trousers mis-clothing my heaving abdomen.

Finally, in my sixties, I found the right person to dress
and undress me: an old illusionist who is able to go behind
a screen in the guise of a cossack and instantly come out at
the other end as

Uncle Sam. He is tasteless ~~and rude, and~~ altogether not a nice person, but he has taught me many a subtle trick such as ~~the~~ folding trousers properly ~~and~~ and I think I shall keep him despite the fantastic wages ~~because wages~~ the rascal asks.

Legs 4 10

Uncle Sam. He is tasteless and rude and altogether not a nice person, but he has taught me many a subtle trick such as folding trousers properly and I think I shall keep him despite the fantastic wages the rascal asks.

Every now and then she would turn up for a few moments between trains, between planes, between lovers. My morning sleep would be interrupted by heartrending sounds — a window opening, a little bustle downstairs, a trunk coming, a trunk going, distant telephone conversations that seemed to be conducted in conspiratorial whispers. If shivering in my nightshirt I dared to waylay her all she said would be "you really ought to lose some weight" or "I hope you transfered that money as I indicated" — and all doors closed again.

Wild remembers

Every now and then she would turn up for a few moments between trains, between planes, between lovers. My morning sleep would be interrupted by heartrending sounds—a window opening, a little bustle downstairs, a trunk coming, a trunk going, distant telephone conversations that seemed to be conducted in conspiratorial whispers. If shivering in my nightshirt I dared to waylay her all she said would be "you really ought to lose some weight" or "I hope you transfered that money as I indicated"—and all doors closed again.

the art of self-slaughter

T L S
16·I·76 " Nietzche argued that the man of
pure will ... must recognise that that there
is an appropriate time to die "

Philip Nikitin:
The act of suicide may be "criminal"
in the same sense that murder is criminal
but in my case it is purified and
hallowed by the incredible delight it gives ⊕.

Notes
the art of self-slaughter

—————————————

TLS 16-1-76 "Nietz[s]che argued that the man of pure
will . . . must recognise that that there is an appropriate
time to die"

Philip Nikitin: The act of suicide may be "criminal" in the
same sense that murder is criminal but in my case it is
purified and hallowed by the incredible delight it gives.

- - - - - - -

By now I have died up to my navel some fifty times in less than three years and my fifty resurrections have shown that no damage is done to the organs involved when breaking in time out of the trance. As soon as I started yesterday to work on my torso, the act of deletion produced an ecstasy superior to anything experienced before; yet I noticed that the ecstasy was accompanied by a new feeling of anxiety and even panic. (More)

Wild D

By now I have died up to my navel some fifty times in less than three years and my fifty resurrections have shown that no damage is done to the organs involved when breaking in time out of the trance. As soon as I started yesterday to work on my torso, the act of deletion produced an ecstasy superior to anything experienced before; yet I noticed that the ecstasy was accompanied by a new feeling of anxiety and even panic.

- - - - - - - - - - - - - - -

¶ How curious to recall the
trouble I had in finding an adequate
spot for my first experiments. There
was an old swing hanging from a branch
of an old oaktree in a corner of the
garden. Its ropes looked sturdy enough;
its seat was provided with a comfortable
safety bar of the kind inherited nowadays
by chair lifts. It had been much used
years ago by my half sister
, a fat dreamy
pigtailed creature, who died before
reaching puberty. I now had to
take a ladder to it, for the sentimental

○

How curious to recall the trouble I had in finding an
adequate spot for my first experiments. There was an old
swing hanging from a branch of an old oaktree in a corner
of the garden. Its ropes looked sturdy enough; its seat was
provided with a comfortable safety bar of the kind inherited
nowadays by chair lifts. It had been much used years ago by
my half sister, a fat dreamy pigtailed creature who died
before reaching puberty. I now had to take a ladder to it, for
the sentimental

relic ~~to~~ was lifted ~~boxed~~ out of human reach
by the growth of the picturesque
but completely indifferent tree. I
had glided with a slight oscillation
into the initial stage of a particularly
rich trance when the cordage
burst and I was hurled, still more
or less boxed into a ditch full of brambles
which zipped off a piece of
the peacock blue dressing gown I
happened to be wearing that summer day.

oo

relic was lifted out of human reach by the growth of the picturesque but completely indifferent tree. I had glided with
a slight oscillation into the initial stage of a particularly rich
trance when the cordage burst and I was hurled, still more
or less boxed[,] into a ditch full of brambles which ripped
off a piece of the peacock blue dressing gown I happened to
be wearing that summer day.

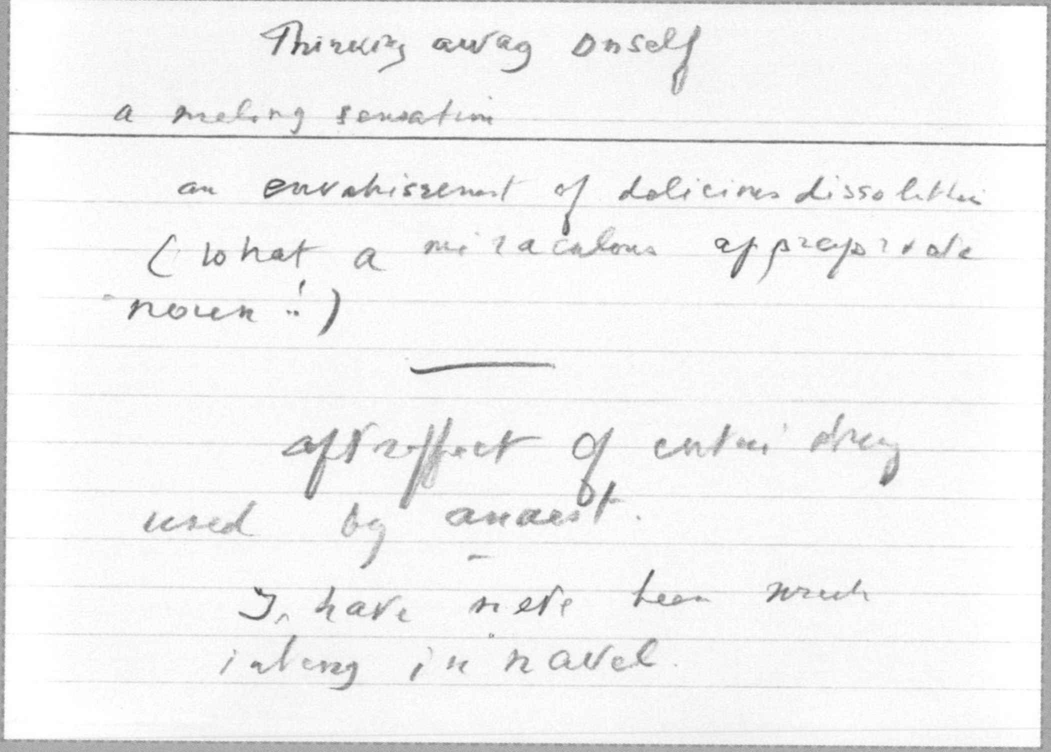

[handwritten note reproduced below]

Thinking away on[e]self
a mel[t]ing sensation
an envahissement of delicious dissolution (what a miraculous appropriate noun!)

aftereffect of certain drug used by anaest[hesiologist]
I have ne[ver] been much [interested] in navel

efface
expunge
erase
delete
rub out
wipe out
obliterate

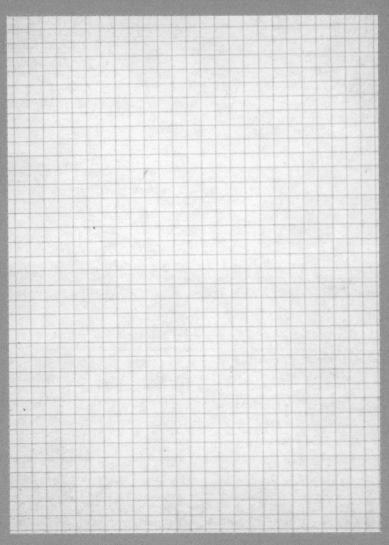

A Note About the Author

Vladimir Vladimirovich Nabokov was born on April 23, 1899, in St. Petersburg, Russia. The Nabokovs were known for their high culture and commitment to public service, and the elder Nabokov was an outspoken opponent of anti-Semitism and one of the leaders of the opposition party, the Kadets. In 1919, following the Bolshevik revolution, he took his family into exile. Three years later he was shot and killed at a political rally in Berlin while trying to shield the speaker from right-wing assassins.

The Nabokov household was trilingual, and as a child Vladimir was already reading Wells, Poe, Browning, Keats, Flaubert, Verlaine, Rimbaud, Tolstoy, and Chekhov, alongside the popular entertainments of Sir Arthur Conan Doyle and Jules Verne. As a young man, he studied Slavic and Romance languages at Trinity College, Cambridge, taking his honors degree in 1922. For the next eighteen years he lived in Berlin and Paris, writing prolifically in Russian under the pseudonym Sirin and supporting himself through translations, lessons in English and tennis, and by composing the first crossword puzzles in Russian. In 1925 he married Véra Slonim, with whom he had one child, a son, Dmitri.

Having already fled Russia and Germany, Nabokov became a refugee once more in 1940, when he was forced to leave France for the United States. There he taught at Wellesley, Harvard, and Cornell. He also gave up writing in Russian and began composing fiction in English. In his afterword to *Lolita* he claimed, "My private tragedy, which cannot, and indeed should not, be anybody's concern, is that I had to abandon my natural idiom, my untrammeled, rich, and infinitely docile Russian tongue for a second-rate brand of English, devoid of any of those apparatuses—the baffling mirror, the black velvet backdrop, the implied associations and traditions—which the native illusionist, frac-tails flying, can magically use to transcend the heritage in his own way." Yet Nabokov's American period saw the creation of what are arguably his greatest works, *Bend Sinister* (1947), *Lolita* (1955), *Pnin* (1957), and *Pale Fire* (1962), as well as the translation of his earlier Russian novels into English. He also undertook English translations of works by Lermontov and Pushkin and wrote several books of criticism. Vladimir Nabokov died in a hospital near Montreux, Switzerland, in 1977.

A Note on the Type

The text of this book was set in Filosofia, a reinvention by type designer Zuzana Licko of the classic Bodoni font. Introduced by the Emigre digital type foundry in 1996, it reduces the contrast of the original's thick and thin strokes for easier reading, while rounding out the ends of the serifs to mimic Bodoni's original letterpress technique. Selected headlines were set in the font's unicase version, which uses a single height for characters that are otherwise separated by upper and lower case, producing an effect that is at once familiar and foreign.

BOOK DESIGN BY CHIP KIDD

Composition and preparation of art by
North Market Street Graphics
Lancaster, Pennsylvania

Printed and bound by
SNP Leefung Printers
China

(DYING IS FUN)